DARA NICHOLS SERIES 1-5

A DARA NICHOLS WORLD NOVELETTE
COMPILATION - VOLUME 2

MARATA EROS

VIP LIST

To be the first to hear about new releases and bargains—from Tamara Rose Blodgett/Marata Eros—sign up below to be on my VIP List. (I promise not to spam or share your email with *anyone!*)

♥ SIGN UP TO BE ON THE MARATA EROS VIP LIST ♥
https://tinyurl.com/SubscribeMarataEros-News
♥ SIGN UP TO BE ON THE TAMARA ROSE BLODGETT VIP LIST ♥
https://tinyurl.com/SubscribeTRB-News

THE SPECIALISTS
A Dara Nichols World Novelette
Volume 3

New York Times BESTSELLER
MARATA EROS

Copyright © 2021 by Marata Eros
All rights reserved.
No part of this book may be reproduced in any form or by any electronic
or mechanical means, including information storage and retrieval systems,
without written permission from the author, except for the use of brief
quotations in a book review.

1

DARA

"THANK YOU, I'LL be there." With a frown, Dara swipes her cell to dark and sighs, shifting her perched weight on a sturdy wooden stool at her kitchen bar.

She loathes the doctor's office. But in the middle of a pandemic, a person must perform certain protocol. If Dara wants to fly down south and have a proper holiday—she must be free of the "big C."

Dara is well-aware of her healthy-as-a-horse status.

But proof is required that she be virus-free three days before flying down south to her favorite resort in Mazatlán, Mexico.

That means a mandatory check-up in the states.

A smile curls Dara's lips as the fine cogs of her mind turn.

University President Taylor has made himself scarce but Dara managed to eke out an additional week of holiday while on her back, Taylor ramming her with his cock. However, this go 'round, it was on her terms. Taylor had gotten schooled by her and Zoe the prior year and Taylor understands who is the dom and who is the sub.

The role reversal had been a sublime triumph for Dara, though she does have to give it up once in awhile.

Not that she objects.

Now that Dara has the green light for extending her Christmas holiday from two to three weeks, she'd coerce a willing girlfriend to ride shotgun.

It wouldn't be Zoe, she and Darrell had gotten serious, and that was a shame.

Dara had loved Zoe's talented tongue.

Picking up her cell again, Dara scrolls through several girlfriend's names.

Darcy—nope, married to a sugar daddy.

Allison? No, too vanilla.

Dara rolls her full lower lip, gnawing pensively on the plump flesh and has a sudden inspiration: *Isabella.*

A beautiful and exotic choice. As blonde as Dara is red, with deep brown eyes and a petite body, Dara remembers a few exciting "events," where Isabella could give as much as she could take.

Dara gives a dark chuckle, relaxing against the backrest of the stool, phone limp on her lap, mentally churning the semantics. Isabella had been up for the "sexcapades," that her and Zoe had manufactured.

Dara was not going to get clit-blocked. She requires a girlfriend who likes to party, get fucked by the gang, and takes care of herself.

Dara likes only the finest horses in the stable.

Nothing ventured, nothing gained, Dara shrugs and swiping her phone awake, she runs an elegant finger over the glass screen, running through the alphabet until she finds the "I's."

Tapping out an economically succinct message, Dara presses *send* and sets her cell on top of the quartz kitchen countertop.

First, the doctor's checkup and a blood test are in order. So *boring*. A sudden thought occurs and Dara smiles, Zoe's been doing some candy striping work at the clinic, maybe Dara will get to see her?

That makes Dara's pussy wet.

How long has it been since Zoe ate her out? Phooey—since Darrell and she got exclusive a few months back.

Maybe Darrell wouldn't be terribly offended if there were to be a little reunion time before she flies the coop for a hotter clime.

And time.

Dara stands, grabbing her cell and making her way to her bedroom.

Lying down on her bed, Dara slowly pulls down her silk boy short loungers, keeping the house at seventy-five degrees so she can wear as little as possible, Dara allows her mind to wander.

Thinking of the first time she let Zoe lick her pussy at the Halloween bash, Dara begins to undulate her hips up and down, remembering with vivid clarity how Zoe had licked and sucked first one side of her labia, then the other.

How the Reaper at the Halloween party had driven the phallus-shaped scythe into Zoe's ass bud while Zoe had eaten Dara's slick cunt and pumped her fingers inside.

With her left hand, Dara widens her pussy lips with thumb and index, exposing her bare clit to the air and groans, taking the memory and making the fantasy real again.

Spreading her legs, she props her cell against her heel and pushes *play* on the video option and lays back down.

Using the tip of her right index finger she begins to whip it across her slick clit, faster and faster, thinking about the shove of Zoe's fingers, the press of her tongue and mouth as she ate Dara, how her face had rhythmically been buried in Dara's wet cunt because she was getting butt-fucked by Reaper and impaled by the scythe in her pussy from behind.

Dara halts the friction on her clit and pumps her finger into her wet channel, pressing hard and fast.

"Aw!" she yells into the room, her pussy becoming full of building pressure.

One. More. Time, Dara thinks. Grabbing the waiting dildo, she hikes her hips high and begins to push the wrist-sized dong inside her waiting pussy. Little by little her channel swallows the girth of the humungous dildo and Dara finally drives it deep, burying the entire length to the hilt in her drenched hole.

The sensation of being completely plugged with the huge cock pushes Dara over the edge and her orgasm crashes through her.

Slowly, Dara pulls the huge cock out of her soaked channel and carefully turns the phone to capture the last perfect pussy pulsing.

A little something for Zoe to think about, Dara muses as she falls back to the bed, calming her breathing as her snatch begs for cock with every pull of empty air.

*

Dara takes a last critical glance at her ensemble. *I'm just going to the doctor's,* she thinks.

Nevermind, Dara's never been great at self-delusion, she is a class-A clotheshorse.

Sky-high heels in screaming crimson are paired with nude hose that run to a garter belt hid by a simple, A-line skirt in jet black. She finishes the outfit with a silk shell blouse that matches the shoes.

Her garter matches the blouse and shoes.

Red is a *no-no* when one is a redhead, but she doesn't care. Dara has a little tinsel in all that redness but nothing a little henna comb-in with conditioner won't keep in check.

Her hair is long and falls to a tapered waist with hips that flare enough to be held. Dara's push up bra offer hers breasts like melons to be tasted.

She hesitates, lingering in front of her reflection for a moment more before deciding against panties.

Dara isn't sure if the exam will require the typical gynecological probe.

Whatever. Dara flounces off, feeling sexy and ready and in a hot mood.

Isabella had replied to last night's text replying she'd *love* to fly to Mazatlan with Dara and she'd get her own testing so she'd be ready.

So ready.

Dara smirks as she grabs her black clutch from the side table that graces her foyer and trots to the door leading to the garage.

Dara's meant for freedom and she intends to take it. Sliding behind the wheel of her Mercedes Benz C-class sedan in a sleek dark charcoal, she presses a button and the keyless engine purrs to life.

Easing out of the garage, Dara makes her way to the clinic she frequents one time a year.

She'll surprise Zoe. That pleases Dara. God knows, Zoe used to *live* to surprise Dara.

Turnaround is fair play.

As she approaches the clinic, Dara removes her cell from

her clutch and slides the Benz into an available spot adjacent to the end of the row.

Scrolling through her phone she finds recent vids and with deft fingers she brightens the cinematography, shortening it to the last, few hot moments of her cunt hunting for cock and presses *save*.

She then scrolls through her contacts, locates Zoe and presses *send*.

Perfect.

Dara exits her car and strides across the empty parking lot with a smug grin.

Let Zoe eat her heart out, since she's not eating me any more.

2

ZOE

ZOE IS BORED as fuck. The candy striper job is just enough to keep her in bread as her and Darrell attempt to figure their shit out. They've been an item for almost a half-year now.

She likes to take advantage of her short breaks between wiping asses, feeding the old peeps and general duties of the mundane.

Zoe pauses over a short TikTok vid, voting on an outfit and throwing her two cents in on some brave bitch that's out there letting people tell her if she looks good or not.

Well if it's not showing cleavage and leg—why bother? *Let's get* all *the attention*, Zoe thinks—not just *part*.

Fucking duh.

Just then an alert pings and Zoe switches over from TikTok vids to text messages.

What? Dara's reached out. With a video. *That's weird.*

It's been ages since they got together to shoot the bull.

Or other things they'd like to shoot at in the past, Zoe thinks with a smirk.

She and D are doing *fine*. Really. But sometimes Zoe

longs for the wild days of the pair of them getting their hot clits off.

Zoe taps the triangle symbol for play and the video begins.

Deep pink pussy lips are spread like a wet flower and the inside of a bright pink vagina is pulsing in rhythmic orgasm.

Zoe does a slow blink. Fuck that's *hot*.

Instantly Zoe recognizes Dara's twat and her panties flood with moisture.

Dara's pussy had been so *fine* to eat. Zoe squirms where she sits, shooting a covert glance around the small dark break room. Seeing no one, she replays the ten-second vid.

Three times.

Finally satisfied, Zoe notices a small message at the bottom.

"Miss me? Because I'll be *coming* soon to your location." After the sentence is a smirking emoticon.

Bitch. What a tease.

Coming soon. *We'll see about that*.

Zoe hops off the single-seater stool and plucking her g-string out of her engorged and drenched pussy she slides her cell in the back pocket of her tight skinny jeans and walks to reception. So she's coming in...?" Zoe feels her brows hike.

Delilah sighs, as unenthusiastic with her job as Zoe. "Nichols, Dara—age forty-one, regular exam plus virus test for upcoming travel." She taps her phone, "Half hourish."

Zoe squeals.

Delilah startles, about dumping her smartphone. "What the fuck, Zo—I think a drop of pee came out."

Zoe laughs but get right on task. "What doctors are working today?"

"Well, Henderson."

Nope, vanilla and little man's syndrome combined, Zoe instantly dismisses.

Delilah runs a finger down her cell screen. "Oh—hey, wait a second."

Zoe impatiently waits, drumming ultra-long crimson nail tips on the elevated reception desk.

"There's a weekly meeting with the intern docs."

The hot, young ones, Zoe immediately translates, *young fresh meat.* Dara can never resist the young stud buffet.

"Brokston, Clark and Meyers." Delilah lifts her chin, meeting Zoe's chocolate gaze.

"Are they almost-doctor dudes?"

She nods. "Yes—they're interns. They're slated to shadow Henderson, but because of the virus, he's the only actual senior doctor. Numbers, you know."

"Drat," Zoe says, deflated.

Delilah's expression turns skeptical. "Are you coming up with one of your schemes?"

Well yeah. Aloud Zoe says, "In a manner of speaking." That's me, coy-as-fuck.

"Whatever you've got going better get happening because Ms. Nichols will be here in a half-hour."

"Are you assisting in my evil plan?"

"Depends."

"Nope. Doesn't *depend.*" Zoe snorts. "Where can I find the young docs?"

Delilah shoots her a long-suffering look and chuckles indulgently. "They're in the conference room waiting for nubby dick Henderson."

Zoe rolls her eyes. *Isn't that the truth.* He's a guy that believes because he's a doctor, a mere candy striper like Zoe should trip over her own feet, ass up and ready to receive his beef fuel injection. Such as that could be.

Ah, no.

Zoe lifts her cell and says, "Text me when Professor Nichols arrives." She winks.

Delilah is suitably impressed. "Teacher huh?"

You have no idea. "Oh she's so much more than that." Zoe waves her palm and begins to walk away with a new purpose, and more than a few tricks up her sleeve.

*

"No way, Ms. Scott." Brokston says, crossing muscular arms over a chest contained within a classic, tight white lab coat. A stethoscope hangs from around his tree trunk neck.

"Come *on*," Zoe says, actually stomping her foot. "She'll be totally into it."

"And we'll have our nuts chopped off," Clark says fist-bumping Meyers midair.

"If we even have nuts *left* after the disciplinary committee gets done with us." Meyers rolls his baby blue eyes, and they're so pretty they should be on a girl, Zoe notes.

"Dara won't sue, she'll just screw your brains out." Zoe pouts, noticing all her hot talk has Brokston's cock in plain outline, rigidly imprisoned inside his chinos.

"You're not totally against the idea," Zoe drawls, running a fingertip over his hidden salami.

He jerks his hips away. "I'm *still* a guy. We must be professional," Brokston says logically. "America's sue-happy. If we even *look* at a woman's tits too long, there will be hell to pay."

Zoe's phone chimes. Delilah has send Dara to the conference room.

Goodie.

"Fuck it. Dara won't sue." Her eyes flash at the three

men, all over six feet, all athletic and decides for them. "What—you guys don't like pussy?" Zoe goads.

"The fuck we don't," Meyers says, actually taking a step toward her.

Her panties get a little wetter.

"Then stop being a sissy, sucking titty baby, and put your dick where your words are."

"You're a hot fucking number," Clark says, eyes darkening as they loosely surround her.

"Taken," Zoe says, lips curling. "But that doesn't mean I can't watch."

Or eat some delicious Dara cream pie, surely Darrell won't mind a little girl on girl action.

As if conjured from thin air, a soft knock sounds on the door. Zoe blazes a warning look at the men and Brokston shakes his head in obvious reluctance.

His prick wasn't reluctant.

We'll win him over, Zoe determines.

She opens the door and Dara's green eyes widen, set off like emeralds by the scarlet blouse. "Zoe," she greets in her contralto drawl.

"Dara." Zoe smiles back. "Listen, loved the little vid." She flutters her black lashes.

Dara's smile broadens into a grin. "I was thinking of you," she begins, voice husky, and seems to suddenly notice the three men behind Zoe, "We have an audience."

"Not for long," Zoe says, towing Dara inside the room by her hand and shutting the door softly behind her.

"What is this?" Dara's slight frown appears as she takes in the men and a long, rectangular conference table anchored in the center of the space.

Zoe turns to the men, sweeping a palm in their direction. "These three interns are specialists."

"Oh?" Dara says coolly, an auburn brow arching. "The specialists," she flicks her tongue along the bottom of her lip as she, clearly contemplating Zoe's words and the men follow the gesture like birds of prey. "In what field of study?"

Brokston hangs back but Meyers steps forward and offers his hand, which Dara takes, obviously anticipating he'll shake it.

Instead Meyers raises her hand to his lips, answering, "Gynecology."

He lays a hot kiss on the back of her hand as their gazes lock.

"Of course," Dara says smoothly, shooting Zoe the narrow look she no doubt deserves.

Dumb.... Dara Nichols is not.

"Are you needing an exam Miss...." Clark asks, his hazel eyes bright with anticipation.

"Professor Nichols," Dara finishes his sentence with subtle correction.

"Never examined a teacher before." Meyers releases Dara's hand and smiles.

Dara's eyes glitter. "Well, there's always a first time to learn something new."

Zoe flips the latch on the door.

3

DARA

DARA CAN'T HELP her involuntary startle at the loud click of the latch and turns to Zoe, eyes narrowed. "I was under the impression we'd have a quick chat as I waited for my appointment."

"I couldn't wait, Dar—thought I'd meet up with your specialists."

Dara studies her recently tamed friend, her dark innocent eyes wide. Zoe is *never* into niceties unless it suits her particular design.

Zoe's always been so *eager*.

She turns her attention to the men, Mr. Gynecology still fluttering about at her right.

There are three men, all hovering in their late twenties.

Dara's most favorite age.

Wetting her lips, she loosely folds her arms, heart beginning to stack up with anticipation beats and plays Zoe's game. "I don't require 'specialists.'"

Zoe has the grace to look slightly embarrassed, her dusky skin flaring with warm deep pink color. "They think you do." She points to the trio of tall handsome drinks of water.

"Ah-huh."

One guy with a vivid blue gaze turns to Zoe—the one Dara has her eye on. "She is not into this, Zoe—and neither am I."

Dara's insides turn molten—she is *all* about the challenge.

"Brokston—" Zoe tries but he waves her off, coming straight for Dara as she stands in front of the only exit—clearly thinking he'll exit.

Dara gives a quick eyes-sweep around the room.

No windows. Perfect.

Dara backs up against the door, pressing her palms flat against the door and props a skyscraper heel against the surface. She bends at the knee high.

Flashing the room her assets.

One of the men sucks in a sharp inhale.

Brokston slows his approach, the click of his throat is loud as he takes the first, hard swallow. "Uh, excuse me Ms. Nichols, I need to get by."

Dara lifts her chin, giving him a bright smile. "Make me."

"Oh my God," she hears one of the men say.

"Yeah," says another.

Mr. Reluctant gives her intense eyes. "I could, you know." His hands flex into fists then release, flex again.

Dara likes his slightly violent vibe. Pushing off from the door, she one-strides into his personal space. Latching on to each side of his stethoscope she drags him down until their noses almost brush. "Then show me what you can do, Brokston."

"Yeah, *show* her," Zoe says like a cheerleading coach.

Brokston hesitates, clearly torn by duty and lust but Dara's seen it all before.

She grips the pole inside his pants and he groans, kicking his head back. "Stop," he grits between teeth.

"No, I believe you don't want me to stop at all," Dara says, pulling him gently by his dick to the conference table.

Dara's eyes run over Zoe as they walk past her, Dara treating her hand like a collar on Brock's cock.

Her focus loops the other two men and she says to Zoe, "You want some?"

Zoe hesitates.

Dara tilts her head to the right, shooting Zoe a look that clearly says, *you began this*. When on earth has Zoe ever *not* come through?

Zoe bites her lip, obviously indecisive.

Fine. Dara ignores her, leading six foot four Brokston by his dick.

Dara backs up until her ass hits the table then releases him.

"We shouldn't do this—we're, I'm—supposed to give you an exam for your flight *plans*, your annual physical doesn't include..."

Dara's lips curl.

He blinks big blue eyes, hair so deep a brown it mimics black.

She fingers her short hem, slowly rolling it to her hips, revealing her scarlet ensemble of garter and panties.

The other pair of doctor's crowds in for a look.

Sweat beads on Brokston's upper lip but he doesn't look away.

Progress.

Dara hikes an ass cheek on the table, widening her leg

and setting her left knee at the edge of the hard surface of the conference table.

The movement displaces her panties perfectly so they bisect her pussy lips.

Brokston follows this with interest.

Dara's grows moist just from watching him fight his instincts.

She gives him guileless green eyes. "I'm clean—and on birth control."

With a low moan, Brokston reaches out and with a trembling finger he caresses her right labia with a delicate stroke.

"Ah," Dara says, shifting just so and her panties move enough to reveal the entrance to her pussy.

Brokston slides his finger into her wet hole, pressing it all the way back. "Fuck, she's sopping wet," he says.

He doesn't seem to be aware that he's withdrawn his finger and cupping her ass cheeks he's slid Dara unto the table until she's lying down flat.

Dara parks her elbows and lifts her upper body slightly, eyeing them—eyeing her.

Zoe moves into Dara's line of sight. "Here," she says softly to Brokston, "here's one of your instruments to examine Dara."

He seems to startle as she hands him a humongous dildo.

Her twat gets wetter. Zoe knows what she likes and this is no different. The length on the phallus is at least ten inches—the girth the size of her wrist.

Size *does* matter, in Dara's estimation.

"That's not..." Clark says, his eyes darkening with lust.

Meyers licks his lips, and clears his throat. "Fuck her with that."

"No—*examine* her," Zoe corrects, voice coy.

"Yeah," Brokston says, giving his head a slight shake as though coming to himself, "I'll do that. Examine."

Dara smirks.

"Let me take her panties off for easier access." Clark rounds the table and pushes in front of Brokston.

Brokston shoves him and Clark staggers back.

The men face off.

Dara looks between the two of them, loving it.

Meyers comes between the pair and Dara nails Brokston in the chest with a well-place spike heel, holding him with a shoe and a look.

His bright baby blues meet her green ones. "Doctor." Dara cocks her head to the left, the fall of her hair moving with the gesture.

Brokston gives a final glance at Clark then stalls out. "Yes."

Dara allows a small frown. "You're all being extremely unprofessional." She pouts. "I. Need. An. Exam."

Brokston large hand encircles one slender ankle, pulling her leg wide as he presses the side of his face against her calf like a cat seeking cream.

Meyers turns, shooting a dark glare at Clark. "*I'll* get the panties off."

Fight over me, Dara thinks, shifting her hips.

Zoe giggles in the background.

Meyers and Brokston close her legs, slowly shimming the panties from her hips and long legs.

The material rasps over her smooth skin and when the fragile material is at the level of her high heels, Meyers plucks them from where they dangle off one heel, finally floating to the ground.

"There, all gone," Clark says like a little boy ready to have his last bite of his favorite food.

Not a bad analogy as those go.

"I want to watch," Zoe says.

She wants to do, If I'm any judge.

Brokston parts her legs, pussy now bare to the men's gazes.

"God," Clark says, look at her glistening hole.

"Tap her with that... examination tool, Brokston," Meyers voice eager with anticipation.

Brokston picks up the huge dong. "Let me check for readiness," he says, and holding the stiff fake cock in his left hand he pierces her drenched cunt with his index finger.

"Yeah," he says, voice shaky, "she's ready for her exam."

Brokston lines up the head of the dong with her entrance and Clark and Meyers hold each of her legs wide.

"Fuck me," Dara growls, needing to be filled with that ginormous appendage.

Brokston begins to press the tapered tip inside her and Dara groans from the sensation of being stretched and owned as he rocks the dildo into her wet pussy.

"Damn, look at her slutty cunt eat that thing," Meyers says wonderingly.

"Just like she'll two time us later."

"For exam purposes only," Brokston qualifies as if he's in a trance.

"Slow down, Brokston," Dara says in a breathy voice.

But he doesn't. Instead, he piston-pumps her cunt as Dara helplessly slides back and forth on the table as he fucks her pussy hard with the thick, hard dildo.

"That's it!" Zoe chimes in, "fuck that cunt!"

Dara's finger finds her clit but it's batted away before she can pleasure herself.

"I need..." Brokston begins.

"To beat off," Clark whispers, eyes trained on the delicacy Dara provides.

Meyers says. "Let me take over."

The men switch and Dara grunts as Meyers pumps into her pussy, keeping the unrelenting rhythm.

Zoe hops onto the table, her jeans gone and a hand between her legs as she fingers her clit as she and Dara are side-by-side.

"What about Darrell?" Dara asks in a whisper.

She gives a tiny head shake. "He won't mind if I eat you, Dara."

Slowly, Zoe leans over Dara and puts her mouth on Dara's clit, flicking the engorged bundle of nerves without mercy.

Meyers slams the cock home and Dara screams inside the room, her orgasm ambushing her from her toes.

Zoe groans against Dara's hot flesh, lapping and sucking her cunt as Dara's pussy pulses around the impaled cock.

Ruthlessly, Meyers drags the big dildo from Dara's pulsating hole and Dara groans at the withdrawal. "Hey!" she cries, wanting more, not near done with the getting the fucking she deserves.

Zoe starts to gasp and writhe against Dara's pussy and Dara knows those sounds intimately.

Zoe's coming. Because she gets off eating Dara out.

"Wait!" Zoe says breathlessly, sliding from the table.

The men caress her sides as she moves past them and Zoe whimpers like an alcoholic denied booze.

Zoe wants to be naughty; but there's Darrell to consider.

She slips in front of the men and bends between Dara's spread legs.

"I've been wanting this," she says.

"Eat my cunt," Dara commands like a queen.

And then Zoe does.

Meyers and Clark smile, but it's Brokston who surprises Dara the most.

"We might have more than one woman who needs a thorough examination," Brokston comments, moving behind Zoe as she plunges her tongue into Dara.

4

DARRELL

"SHE'S NOT GETTING the message," Darrell gripes to Kev, slapping his cell on his thigh.

Kev shrugs. "Fuck it."

"I mean—she hasn't *seen* the message." Darrell gazes at his cell, watching the filled-in checkmark that clearly shows the message was successfully sent and received, but no little circle that contains Zoe's smiling face is present.

"You don't think a surprise is in order?" Kevin drawls, draining half his water bottle, crushing and tossing the mashed plastic in the recycling can at the corner of the weight room.

Darrell's big hands hang loosely between his legs. He's resting between his second to last rep on of his final set.

"Yeah," he replies slowly to Kev. "We get done with this last rep and then I'm going to have a chat with my girl."

One of Kevin's dark eyebrows drives up. "What kind of chat?"

Darrell rakes a hand over his skull cap of hair. "Think she's stepping out on me."

Kev jerks his chin back. "Nah, man—Zoe promised she was hanging up the 'ho angle and being a one-man woman."

Darrell clenches his jaw, feeling the flutter appear from his tension. "Zoe's not as happy in the sack anymore."

Kev chuckles. "Sounds like that's a personal problem, bud. Yours."

Probably. Darrell shoots him a stiff middle finger. "Maybe it's my turn to offer some spice."

"What about your needs?" Kevin whips the hand towel he just used to wipe the sweat off his face around his neck, holding onto the ends with his hands.

Firefighters eat together, workout together and sometimes, like what happened a few months ago at the firehouse—they fuck together.

Me and Kev have been through some shee-it.

His next exhale is raw. "She hung up 'ho life for me but I don't know if she was a hundred percent *into* the decision."

"If it's bugging your ass so much, go figure it out. She's gets breaks at the clinic, right?"

Darrell nods. "That's just the thing. It's her lunch hour—she *should* be seeing my messages."

Kev and me exchange a glance. "What about that classy redhead she was banging the world with?"

"Dara?"

Kevin nods.

"She's around, they don't hang out so much anymore. When Zoe stopped getting off with her, they saw less of each other."

"So this Dara is a bad influence?" Kev spreads his arms away from his body.

Darrell snorts. "The worst."

Zoe

ZOE FEELS FIRM, large hands on her ass. Like—she notices the sensation, but right now, with Dara's wet splayed cunt in her face, Zoe's all about *the moment*.

Until she feels a hard something at her entrance.

Zoe lifts her face from Dara's pussy. "Hey!" she says loudly.

Eating Dara is one thing, but she'd promised Darrell she won't bang anyone else.

Dara doesn't count.

Brokston says breathlessly, "Hold her face against that redheaded pussy."

What. The. Fuck? Zoe has time to think, before Clark has beefed her face into Dara's pussy.

Suffocating her.

Dara bucks her hips and Zoe sucks in air, and a bunch of yummy pussy juices to boot as she tries to claim some oxygen.

"Relax Zoe, you wanted to eat this cunt so *eat it*."

Zoe starts lapping at Dara again, tilting her face like a swimmer seeking air and Clark's hand at her nape eases. But not the thing being stabbed into her wet hole.

She's always liked a little dubcon action and this *so* qualifies. Zoe can't help what she does next, making little contented pig noises as she slides her hands beneath Dara's small ass cheeks and goes to town on her twat.

"Wow, look at her eat the snatch buffet," she recognizes Meyers voice.

"And Brok is having so much fun using the tool Zoe provided to get herself nailed." He chuckles.

"These sluts *like* their exam," Meyers says.

Zoe groans at the intrusion of the huge dong that's already been inside Dara as pummels her moist center.

Zoe tips her pelvis up, taking as much as she can get of that stiff length and Brokston obliges, shoving it in as fast and deep as her body can accept the size.

"Ah!" Zoe calls out, whipping her head back as she swivels her hips to accept more.

"Plug her!" Clark shouts, cracking the air with a handclap.

"I have to be thorough," Brokston replies in a clinical voice, shoving the dildo to the hilt.

He drags the dildo from Zoe and she spreads her legs further, beginning to play with her clit.

Brokston slams it home.

Zoe screams at the massive surge inside her pussy, whipping her finger over her slick clit, feeling that delicious pressure begin to build within her core.

"Eat me, Zoe," Dara instructs.

Zoe bends over, taking the abusive fucking and playing with herself as she laps at Dara's cunt, then tongue fucks her. Zoe's breaths become ragged pants that saw in and out.

"Fuck me you selfish bitch," Dara commands.

Zoe's face keeps smashing against Dara's pussy because Brokston is fucking her hard with the dildo.

Her finger sweeps a final lash over her clit and Zoe's suddenly coming hard, pulsing around the dildo in huge rhythmic clenches.

Zoe's writhing, the cock slamming her from behind as Dara's juices drip from her chin. Zoe's self-possessed enough to fist her small hand and start shoving inside Dara.

Dara grunts at the sensation, spreading her legs as the

specialists take flanking positions, Clark holding one slim leg down and Meyers the other.

Dara's going to get filled if it's the last thing I do.

"That's right, give me all of it," Dara moans as Zoe begins to drive her fist inside Dara's hot cunt as Zoe's pussy still pulses around the dong.

Dara lifts her hips, assisting Zoe's fucking of her.

Zoe pushes and pulls fucking Dara's soft, wet cunt with her closed fist.

The wet sucking sound of Dara's pussy getting punished makes Zoe's pussy get drenched and her hoo-hah accepts the dong all the way, Brokston pounding it deep.

Dara bellows.

Zoe grins, going deeper inside Dara's drenched hole.

"God that's hot, look at that dirty whore take her friend's fist," Zoe hears Clark say.

Both men have their cocks in hand, fingers wrapped hard and driving them up and down the length of their huge erections.

"Stick it in her mouth," Meyers says from Zoe's left, "Don't forget to make sure you give her the tongue depressor as part of her *exam*."

God, they're going to come in her, Zoe thinks, her pussy juice beginning to run down her inner thighs as Brokston moves her body back and forth with his expert rocking inside her twat.

Dara takes it out of everyone's hands, grabbing each cock, she pulls the men down low.

Clark straddles her, his assbud in full view of Zoe as the dong keeps her seesawing nearer.

He lowers himself toward Dara's full lips, pushup-style and she guides his cock into her mouth.

Clark's ass cheeks clench as he starts to softly fuck her mouth, but Zoe knows he'll never last.

No one ever can with Dara.

Zoe pushes her fist high as another sensation of penetration begins at her asshole.

Zoe squirms as her ass begins to get stuffed with something hard. She can't move., between Clark using his free hand on the back of her neck, and her pussy impaled by the dong from behind—she can't keep her promise to Darrell as the men own her holes and she owns Dara's.

Dara gurgles around Zoe's fist plugging her pussy as Clark begins to unload his cum in her mouth.

Dara's throat works, swallowing his load down, Clark gagging her with his length.

Dara tries to move but Zoe's fist is buried and a dick impales her throat.

"Move out of the way," Meyers says, voice ragged.

He pushes Clark off the table and he and his flaccid cock go down hard, hitting the floor with an elbow crack and he bellows.

Dara turns her head, cum leaking from her lips and chokes, more comes out and her body convulses around Zoe's fist.

Zoe fucks her harder.

"Ah, Zoe!" she says helplessly as Meyers does a final jerk and pull of his cock, he fists her hair and shoves her face down his shaft, throwing his head back he howls, hips tight and forward as he dumps a second load of cum into Dara's waiting mouth.

The pressure that was building crescendos, exploding— the scene of Dara so fucking hot Zoe's helpless as she begins to come again, the dual swords are invading length in both her holes as Brokston fucks her hard.

Zoe's so invested in the invasion from behind and the wet pussy in front, she doesn't hear the door slam open until it's too late.

Darrell's voice booms, momentarily yanking Zoe out of her dazed sexual fugue of lust.

5

DARRELL

THE SOUND OF wet pounding reach him and that just amp his shit up.

Zoe's in there.

Darrell reaches forward and tries the door handle, finding it locked.

Fuck *this*.

Stepping back, Darrell plants his right foot behind him and with a small hop, he whips his leg forward, striking just to the left of the door handle and the metal slab flies inward, slapping the wall and swings back.

He arrests the door with his hand and takes in the scene.

Three guys have their naked Johnson's in their hands, eyebrows-up in clear shock at his sudden appearance while a half-naked Zoe has half her arm buried in Dara's pussy.

As his eyes sweep behind Zoe, some dude has plugged her holes with a double-the-fun-dildo.

Darrell sees red.

Zoe removes her arm from Dara's snatch and tries to wiggle out of reach from the guy that Darrell goes for first.

Darrell's a firefighter, and at six foot two and two-hundred twenty pounds of lean fighting machine, he's built to met damage.

"Fuck!" the guy behind Zoe bellows and stumbles back, leaving the dong hanging from Zoe.

"Darrell!" Zoe shrieks.

Too late.

Darrell two-strides it, nailing Mr. Impaler in the head.

His jaw snaps back and he falls.

The two other dudes who'd been flanking Dara come at him.

Gives new meaning to swinging dicks.

Darrell gives a hard love tap to the dude who was driving his cock in Dara's mouth just seconds ago and he gives an abbreviated squealing pig noise and sinks, hands at his crotch as his knees tap the ground.

The other guy clocks Darrell in the shoulder, missing the target of his jaw.

Darrell backhands him in a slap so hard the fucker staggers backward, planting his naked ass on the unforgiving hospital floor.

"Well, well," Dara says, spreading her legs, dark green eyes glittering her invitation.

The sight of her bright pink, well-used hole gets his full attention.

A wet thunk sounds from his left and it's Zoe—she's finally gotten the dong out of her cunt and tossed it on... the guy who put it there. His light snores would be funny if the gooey dong decorating his chest hadn't just been fucking his girl.

Yeah, that.

Darrell ignores Zoe and goes directly for Dara.

Two can play at this game.

Darrell unbuckles his pants, kicking them from one leg

and then the other, dropping them as he walks to where Dara lies on top of a long conference-type table.

Dara doesn't say no, sliding her cherry red stilettos to the table's edge and baring more of her best part.

He slides his hands beneath her tight ass and lines up the erection he's sporting at her wet hole.

Dara lifts her hips and his hands convulse on her butt cheeks. "Come on, big boy."

Darrell doesn't pause, beginning to slide his stiff length inside of her drenched pussy.

Zoe warmed her up for him and there's no resistance as he fills her with his huge cock.

Darrell's inky skin contrasts with Dara's alabaster paleness where a trimmed tuft of bright red curls top her pink slit.

He doesn't hold back, stabbing his black meat into her pale, hungry pussy.

"Oooh, Darrell!" Dara says breathlessly, "drive it deep!"

Darrell leans over, exposing his bare ass to the room as he drives his cock to the hilt.

"Bastard," a feminine voice says from behind him as something long and hard begins to shove inside his asshole.

"Hey!" he yells at the intrusion, but deep down, Darrell likes his ass plugged while he's hammering pussy and he widens his legs, allowing more penetration.

Whoever's doing the fucking doesn't take it easy on him and Darrell's ass protests the abuse.

As though the fucker senses it, Darrell feels the cool sensation of lube and doubles down on Dara's twat, ramming into her like he's mining for China.

"This is what you get for fucking my friend," Zoe says and the dildo pumps, each stroke harder than the last.

Darrell can't last and with a final grunt, he slams his cock home into Dara's soaked cunt and lets his load go at the same time he feels a wet sensation and realizes the truth.

That wasn't a dildo up his ass.

It was a guy's thick cock.

∼

Zoe

ZOE LOVES DARA.

What she doesn't love is Darrell showing up and making a bunch of assumptions and then without even glancing her way he begins fucking Dara.

Dara.

How is that fair? Zoe was eating Dara and fisting her—no big—Darrell would have totally been on board with some girl-on-girl action.

But *no.*

Instead, he comes in here like he's *all that,* busts the chops of the dudes and begins fucking her friend.

Well Zoe's got news for *him.*

She waits until he's hammering Dara and grabs the dong off Brokston.

Sneaking up behind him, Zoe starts stuffing the dong inside his ass.

Zoe knows that Darrell secretly likes an ass-fucking and wedges it inside.

When Meyers gets up from the floor he puts a finger to his lips in the universal *silence* signal.

Zoe has to hold back a laugh, isn't this just turning out *fine.*

Darrell is totally absorbed by pistoning inside Dara and Zoe's keeping the ass-fucking going.

When Meyers grabs some lube from his doctor's smock pocket, Zoe grabs his bare cock and begins moving her hand up and down.

Meyer's pours lube over his cock as she jacks him off.

When he's lubed and stiff as fuck—Zoe slides the dildo from Darrell's hot ebony hole and Meyers begins to dip his wick.

At first Meyers uses no hands and just drives his hips forward, plunging inside Darrell as he rocks inside Dara.

Zoe cruises around the table as Darrell bellows, clearly orgasming inside Dara.

She nods to Meyers and he dives forward, taking advantage of Darrell's orgasming to return the favor. Pumping fast and hard Meyer's grabs Darrell's hips and holding him still, he buries his cock in Darrell's ass.

Meyers stiffens, cords standing in stark relief at his thick throat as he comes inside Darrell with a raw exhale of lust.

Darrell drops forward, attempting to withdraw his cock from Dara. That proves impossible because Meyers isn't quite finished with Darrell's ass.

Zoe's in the forward position of Darrell.

Their eyes meet.

"Thanks for fucking Dara."

Without missing a beat Darrell says, "Thanks for fucking the three dudes here."

Meyers pulls out of Darrell's ass and a sliding line of cum begins to trail down the inside of his leg.

"Looks like you're all about getting fucked or fucking if *you're* the one doing it."

Zoe's chest is tight. It was exciting to eat Dara, and she wasn't looking for a hook-up with the docs.

Brokston just took advantage of her position, and it'd been pretty fun. Technically she wasn't fucking a guy.

Brokston was an opportunist.

Meyers too. He didn't bat an eyelash about fucking Darrell's ass.

But Darrell crossed the line.

Zoe looks to Dara and she turns her head and says, "Come on Zo, you're not going to let a little bit of fucking get in the way of a great time."

Maybe Zoe's just not as opportunistic as some of her nearest and dearest.

Like Dara.

Like Darrell.

"I think I'll take myself outta here about now."

"Zoe," Dara says, hiking herself up on the table and attempting to drag her short skirt down over her slippery parts, "wait."

"Nope," Zoe says, trying like hell not to cry and failing as she swipes at her eyes. "God knows I dig a good time. What I *don't* like is my *supposed* boyfriend showing up, assuming shit and fucking my best friend and allowing himself to get fucked by whoever, while I *watch*."

"Zoe," Darrell says, standing with a small grimace and giving her a contrite look then giving Meyers side-eye juju.

She shakes her head, walking by a groaning Brokston and jerking her pants off the floor she moves toward the door.

"You can have your next exam on your own, Dara." And with that, Zoe goes to the wrecked door and walks out, leaving the doctors and Dara and Darrell to sort their shit.

TONGUE DEPRESSOR
A Dara Nichols World Novelette
Volume 4

New York Times BESTSELLER
MARATA EROS

Copyright © 2021 by Marata Eros
All rights reserved.
No part of this book may be reproduced in any form or by any electronic
or mechanical means, including information storage and retrieval systems,
without written permission from the author, except for the use of brief
quotations in a book review.

6

ZOE

THAT FIREDICK MOTHER *fucker,* Zoe internally rants.

Swiping her tears, she frog marches her ass to the dressing rooms where the work lockers are located.

She punches open the door and lets it swing shut with an echoing slam.

Navigating between central wooden benches bisecting the rows of lockers on either side Zoe comes to stand in front of her locker.

Dragging off her drawstring pants, smock top (that actually has an allover print of unicorns pissing rainbows) Zoe dumps the load on the floor, stares at the dirty clothes for a second and kicks it against the base of her locker for good measure.

Her exhale is raw anger. *Dara.*

Zoe lifts her arm and sneers at the remnants of drying pussy juice.

That *hoe.*

With a snort of disgust, Zoe strides to the open trough of

showers and stepping onto the cool tile she jerks on the first tap she sees to scalding, *fuck tepid.*

Backing up into the hot spray she grabs the community soap and begins the lathering process, so stinking pissed she can't form a coherent thought.

And to think that Zoe was excited about seeing Dara and imagining all the potential sexcapades that could unfold with the right circumstance in place.

She even had the interns involved.

Zoe's honeypot gets a little wet thinking about that double dipping dong. That was *fun* as fuck.

There won't be any more of *that,* though.

Tipping her head back, Zoe lets the hot water soak her hair and without opening her eyes, tries to braile out the shampoo bottle she'd set beside the soap that's always at the ready.

Instead, she touches a hand and yelps.

Jumping back, she blinks her soaked eyelashes apart.

Brokston stands there. "Your in the wrong locker room, pal," Zoe wraps a protective arm around her boobs and jerks her thumb toward the door where Mr. Big Dick and Handsome just slithered through.

He can fuck off too.

Zoe loves the way he impaled her with the double-dildo fun, when she was eating Dara's twat, but that doesn't mean he can ramrod his ass in here when she's mentally licking her emotional wounds and just stand there all naked and delicious.

Or can he?

Zoe tries to give him an indifferent assessment. Her eyes running the length of his nakedness.

Wait, he's not naked. He's still got his doctor's pants on, only his chest is bare.

Her eyes latch onto the stethoscope that dangles around his thick neck.

Zoe swallows, hard.

Just because Darrell cheated on her, and was an assumptive dickhead doesn't mean she needs to just panty-drop because Brokston shows up looking all eatable.

Uh-huh.

"I wanted to apologize," he breaks through her thoughts.

What, for Meyers butt-fucking my cheating boyfriend? Zoe thinks uncharitably. After all, Meyers saw a hot dark hole and took advantage while Zoe helped.

Zoe likes helping.

Meyer's isn't really at fault and neither is Brokston. If she's fully honest, Zoe's the one who choreographed the entire event, without knowing Darrell would do the surprise visit.

Her and Darrell's suitcase of emotional bullshit is theirs.

"It's okay," Zoe says, trying to keep the sullen out of her voice and failing bigtime.

"You liked it when Meyers was nailing the black stallion."

Zoe's eyes flick to the semi-hardon that is beginning to tent his doc pants.

Looks like Brokston was a fan too. *Focus, Zoe.* She gets back on track, slapping her bare thighs. "Of *course*, I did!"

Brokston stares down at her with bright blue eyes framed by inky-black eyelashes.

She's always been a sucker for baby blues.

Brokston steps closer, and with a gentle finger, he plucks a tendril of soaked hair and flicks it behind her shoulder.

Zoe's breath catches.

"I didn't want you to misunderstand. We thought

everyone wanted to play, who was in the room. The redhead certainly did. And when your boyfriend—"

"Darrell," Zoe inserts tightly.

"Yes—when Darrell showed up, he joined in right away and started *examining* our patient. Seemed like she wanted a *thorough* exam."

Dara likes thorough.

Brokston's eyes hood. "You weren't cheating on your boyfriend because we used a toy to examine you while you... made sure our patient was getting proper *treatment*."

"No," Zoe agrees softly, "I didn't mind my exam," her voice lowers to a whisper, "I just promised my boyfriend there wouldn't be any more men."

Brokston shakes his head and spreads heavy arms away from his body. "There hasn't been any other men. Not really."

Zoe finds herself distracted by his Adam's apple.

Then Brokston slides his pants down.

"Hey!" Zoe gasps, eyes instantly glued to his impressive junk. "You're not allowed to shower in the women's dressing room."

Brokston's pale blue eyes gleam.

"Are you going to say no?" His dark eyebrows rise. "I thought I'd apologized and we'd come to an understanding that you had not cheated and that you'd been assisting our patient." Brokston's hand goes to his chest in innocence.

He's good, Zoe thinks.

"Besides," Brokston says, "I feel a little *used,* if you get my meaning. I'd like to freshen up."

"Okay," Zoe says.

Brokston kicks off his pants and they fly off with a final flick of his ankle, landing just outside the border of the wet tile.

His naked butt cheeks bunch and release as Brokston turns his back on her and walks to the opposite shower head ten feet from where Zoe stands transfixed, water sluices between her shoulder blades.

Brokston grabs the soap and laboriously lathers until there's nothing but fragrant froth hiding those large, strong hands.

He begins to wash his chest, deft fingers sliding over a broad, heavily muscled pec then transferring to the other.

His nipples harden from the contact as he works lower and the suds succumb to gravity, luscious soap trailing the muscled contours of his abs.

When Brokston gets to his cock and balls, Zoe breathing becomes labored.

Fuck.

Brokston keeps scooping and pulling his prick and the rod of flesh hardens—gorgeous, long and... wet.

Their eyes meet and her heartbeats pile up like pancakes.

"Will you do my back, Ms. Scott?" he drawls.

I'll do more than that, Zoe thinks, moving from the spray and welcoming the chill of the air.

7

DARRELL

"WAIT—DARRELL!!" DARA calls loudly. The click of heels chime behind him but he doesn't turn as he makes his way toward the door.

Of course, he's aware his behavior is a fucked-up way to treat Dara because things went pear-shaped with him and Zo.

Reluctantly, Darrell turns, folding his arms across his broad chest.

His eyes move behind Dara for a sec. The doctors reassembling their pricks in their pants isn't distracting At. All.

Nope.

Or the fresh memory of them taking turns on his asshole.

Good thing his skin is ebony or the heat of his embarrassment would be on full display.

As it is, bravado and Academy Award acting will have to get him through this fine moment.

His attention returns to Dara, who appears a little rough

around the edges. Cum has dried on her bright red skirt and the ankle strap on one of her red stilettos has been torn off.

The visual curls his lips.

"Listen—Zoe didn't participate on any one-on-one fun."

I did. "But you and me," I jab a thumb in the center of my chest, "we fucked-it-out."

Her green eyes rise to meet his brown ones, red hair swirls around tits that peek from above a black lacy bra. "Zoe will forgive us." Dara lifts a slender shoulder. "After all, this is the least of the activities she and I have participated in together. There's a *long* history of fun."

His eyes flick to the two docs behind Dara. "Private discussion."

They ignore his not-so-subtle dismissal. "I'm Meyers and this is Clark," Meyers says then his expression turns sheepish. "Hey man—thought you were on board with everything." He spreads his hands away from his sides.

"These doctors were giving me a thorough exam for my upcoming holiday." Dara cocks a dark auburn brow significantly.

Darrell gets the game; one hundred percent. "*I* didn't need an exam."

Not that Darrell minded being plugged exactly....

Clark smirks, hazel eyes brimming with mirth. "I didn't hear a *no* anywhere in here during our exam."

Truth. *Fuckers.*

I've got to find Zo and figure this out. He'd made her—forced Zo into monogamy, so now it's up to Darrell to come to her—hat in hand—and be the one to do the apologizing.

He was tag-teamed. And not only did Darrell *love* what happened, sliding his horse-dick into Dara's redheaded snatch, but getting his backend pipe cleaned in the process.

"Go find Zoe and explain your part in all this," Dara urges, eyes earnest.

"What *is* my part?"

Dara smirks, crossing her arms beneath her impressive rack and hiking it with the gesture. "The part where you came in and attacked the docs because you saw Zoe getting a double-dipper and assumed the situation."

Darrell's sigh is raw, exhausted. Because mentally, he's tired of all this.

"You know—you might want to consider letting Zoe have her fun. She's not a white picket fence sort of girl and I don't think she's ever going to be one." Dara flips a palm out then turns it, pointing at him.

Damn.

He's been sorta thinking that way somewhere in the back of his brain, hadn't he? Zoe will be his, she'll calm down, she'll like their scene, blah, blah, blah.

Instead, he's just holding her back from all the juicy shit she obviously likes to sample.

Has a taste for.

Then Darrell came in and fucked it up by banging Dara and whacking a few heads together—not in that order.

Decision made, Darrell knows Dara's right.

With a final glance at the two smirking twin docs, Darrell pivots, heading for the door.

Maybe Delilah will see what direction Zo took off in?

∽

Z~

ZOE'S MOUTH WATERS. He's *tall*.

So tall that her head barely comes to his shoulder.

Zoe licks her lips. "Hey," she softly calls out.

Brokston whips around, his big cock softly slapping her thigh and Zoe sucks back a sharp inhale.

"Sorry," Brokston says, "I know you're trying to stay away from other men."

Clearly an epic fail. Zoe clears her throat, forcing eye contact. "You said you wanted me to do your back?"

His smile is slow and spreads over a handsome face, beautiful blue eyes darkening with lust.

"Yes. My *back*," he repeats, in a deadpan voice.

As he turns to show her his back, Zoe glances at his huge cock and gulps.

Back. *Back.* Backity-back-back.

His large hands brace against the tile as the water from the shower head lashes his broad back and he leans over.

Huge balls and a slightly parted ass bud open for her perusal.

Back.

When his free hand shows up between his legs with a chubby cube of soap inside Zoe must reach between his legs to grab the semi-slick bar, brushing his nutsack as she moves.

Oh my God.

Brokston's azure eyes meet hers briefly over his shoulder. "I'll keep forward like this so you can get all my dirty bits, Ms. Scott."

Zoe's pussy floods with moisture at his naughty instruction.

She likes to clean.

Like a good girl, Zoe takes the soap, wetting the square chunk where some of the shower spray hits her naked breasts and begins to lather until the foamy goodness is dripping down her forearms.

"I'm ready."

Brokston's chuckle is muted. "I bet you are."

Oh God. Zoe begins at the top of his broad shoulders, gently kneading and working her way down to the upper middle of his back.

Brokston hangs his head, groaning in pleasure. "That's nice, reaaalll nice, Ms. Scott."

Zoe reaches the dimples at his lower back and hesitates.

"Please, Ms. Scott—I think I need a thorough washing of all the bits that I can't reach."

"Okay," Zoe says, voice breathy.

Her fingers slide over the firm curve of his perfectly-shaped ass cheeks... and slide inside his ass, parting the smooth, muscular globes.

"I'll just clean this part here." Her two fingers rim his ass bud and she moves further inside, piercing his ass with a fingertip.

She sinks to her knuckle, the suds allowing smooth penetration.

"Oh yeah, get me squeaky-clean," Brokston says, voice tight.

Zoe keeps the backdoor action up and with her other hand she reaches between his legs, cupping his balls and running her hand allover his nutsack.

Brokston groans at her precise attention.

Zoe loves clean balls.

She's unsurprised when she makes her way to his long cock that the length of flesh is fully erect.

A hot rod for her hand to squeeze.

Zoe begins to work her sudsy hand up and down the girth, subtly popping off the top and driving her palm back down the entire shaft.

Pressing her breasts against Brokston's back she cups his

body, adding another finger to the butt-fucking she's giving him.

Oh! She mentally updates—*the cleaning of his tight anus.*

Ramming a second finger in his clenched ass summons another moan and his butt channel tenses around her pumping digits.

Zoe smiles. This is a *fine* cleaning.

Her left hand tightens on his prick, moving fast now as her right hand fingers keep up their plunging assault.

"Don't stop cleaning me!" Brokston yells into the empty locker room his body bucking to assist Zoe's rhythm.

She's jerking his junk abusively when he stiffens, shouting into the shower spray he calls out her name, "Ms. Scott!"

Zoe peeks around his body, slowing her pace and enjoys the show as hot jets of cum pump out the end of his dick and slap the tile in front of them, mixing with the soap and water as the yum slides down the moist wall.

Brokston has clean parts, she thinks, an amused smile overtaking her face.

"So this is staying away from other men?" Darrell's low voice reaches Zoe.

Fuck. Releasing Brokston's big dick and removing her fingers out of Brokston's deelish ass, Zoe slowly turns.

Darrell's hurt and rage-filled expression meets hers and a few seconds of silence pound by.

Well. Fuck. *Him.*

Just then Brokston has apparently turned to face forward because he wraps his arms around Zoe's body then cups her large breasts with his hands, saying in a low satisfied purr, "Don't be mad, Darrell—your girl was just cleaning my parts, as I requested."

Darrell expression gradually morphs from one of anger

to one of determination. "Well I'm sure she's dirty as fuck," he growls.

Zoe can hear the smile in Brokston's voice. "Well let's clean her up then."

Darrell smile flashes like a shark smelling blood. "Together."

Brokston hooks his arms underneath Zoe's pits and Darrell strides toward her.

Maybe Zoe bit off more than she could chew.

8

D~

ZOE SQUIRMS IN Brokston's hold and for once, Darrell's glad he isn't the one having to orchestrate the fun—and it delays the inevitable.

This is all on Zo.

She set up this bullshit with Dara and her "exam." Hell—it was Zoe's fault that Darrell had to get off with Dara because Zo was all into the double dong.

He's just about got himself convinced of not needing to apologize when Zoe says, "Maybe I don't want you cleaning me, D."

What. In. The. Absolute. Fuck, his mind shrieks.

Darrell's fists clench.

Zoe spreads her legs, giving him a peek of the goods, the cunning wench.

His eyes cruise over her hot pink pussy—from his vantage point, ready and willing.

Her eyes take in his expression and the corners of Zoe's lips twitch. "You have to *kiss* and *makeup* now, Darrell. Me sticking my fingers up Brokston's tight ass does *not* mean 'gettin with' other men. I'd say you banging away at Dara—is definitely getting after *other* women."

Darrell had been all ready to apologize but he walked in on Zoe thrusting her fingers up some other dude's back door and lost all the gumption.

Sex is a slippery slope. It's not just about sticking your dick in a hole. Sometimes, it's about sharing sexual stuff with somebody else. But Darrell's big thing had been Zoe not doing none of that crank with any other dudes.

He'd have to reevaluate a Dara, chick-on-chick thing.

Darrell slows his stride to Zo, crossing his beefy arms across his muscular chest. He ain't shy about his looks. He knows he looks as good as a guy who works constantly can. Now that Darrell has moved up the ranks of the firehouse ladder, he's getting decent time off, spending it with Zo or lifting with Kevin.

Women. *Damn.*

Zoe's breasts jiggle as she moves within Brokston's hold. "I see those fine mental wheels turning. But ya can't take back the pause, baby—you're not into being sorry, not really. You busted into my scene with Dara, assumed a bunch of trumped-up shit, thunked heads then banged her to spite me." She reaches backward, winding her arms around Brokston's neck and arching her back.

Darrell's eyes latch onto her enormous thrusting tits.

That's about right—all of it and he's not crazy about how she explained it all; hits a bit too close to home.

He glares at Zo, and Brokston cups her butt cheeks, hiking her off the ground and she widens her legs as Brokston spreads her midair.

Darrell licks his lips. He knows that pussy, inside and out. Literally. It's like a comfort food.

Comfort twat.

His eyes flick to that juicy, wet open flower. He wants to devour her.

Just then Dara and the two docs waltz in.

But Darrell's indecision costs him.

Dara always has a scheme and this is no exception. With a sultry smile, her eyes take in the scene and she throws the latch on the door. "If there's any females, they can use the boy's room," she announces with conviction.

Darrell gives her a sour look. *Hardy-har-har.*

Dara breezes past him with barely an acknowledgement, then suddenly turning, she grabs his face with her hand and makes a blowfish mouth by squeezing his lips together. "Darrell's all whah-baby?" she asks lightly.

She drops her hand, dismissing him and walks over to Zo. "Hello, my lovely," she coos.

It's clear by Zoe's unenthused expression she's in zero mood to be pacified, looking away with a defiant chin hike.

Dara places her slender hands on her hips, and snaps her fingers in the air like she's hailing a cab.

Meyers and Clark come a running.

Executing a smooth pivot to Meyers at her left she says, "Zoe has only had a *partial* exam. And what with Isabella and myself leaving on holiday shortly, I believe it's her turn. And you *must* be thorough." She bats her deep copper eyelashes. "I'm counting on you two."

"It's *not* my turn," Zoe counters, her dusky complexion warms to pink as her cheekbones color.

Darrell's girl is getting all fired-up..

"My arms are tired," Brokston admits, "with all this wasted time arguing about *feelings.*"

Dara's dark forest green eyes narrow at the pair. "Precisely my point. Examinations from professionals don't matter. Feelings do not enter in to the current situation."

She juts out a fine hip and Darrell notices the skirt has gone MIA between the "examination room" and the women's changing room and Dara is decorated with only a g-string.

No surprise there.

"Yes," Brokston agrees, clearly a Dara enthusiast.

Brokston lowers Zoe to her feet and she huffs, shooting Darrell a withering glance.

Turning to Dara, a naked Zoe accuses Dara, "You just had to bang Darrell."

Dara gives an elegant shrug, staying classy despite being in underwear and wearing heels worse-for-wear.

"I don't admit to the banging, though I was happy to be the bangee." She gives a breathy snigger. "And of course, Darrell entered our exam room at the precise time I was clamoring for a thorough look-see."

Zoe snorts. "You'd take a look-see from anyone," she mutters.

Dara acts as though she's thinking about Zoe's insight for a moment. "Too true. Your point?"

Zoe gives a soft laugh. "I can't stay mad at you, ya skank."

Dara's lips curl. "I'm aware. The potential for fun is limitless, my dear, sexy friend. Don't spoil things because your black stallion has arrived and feels as though he has to pee in the corners."

What? "Hey!" He says, gearing up for the defense angle.

Dara's steady green eyes shift to him. "Quiet, Darrell—you've had your fun." Dara rotates in his direction and with great precision and hooks her fingers at the material on her hips, beginning the slow pull of the sexy lace panties down her smooth body.

Of course, her heels are so high that balance is key. As soon as Dara gets wobbly, Meyers steps forward, holding her elbow as she bends over and flicks the panties from her high-heeled foot.

They land in a silky black pile at Darrell's feet.

Zoe's eyes roam his expression and she giggles. "D looks sucker-punched."

Dara's sultry chuckle joins hers.

With all the naked ladies around, it's difficult to keep your head on straight.

Darrell notices Dara doesn't straighten, but remains bent over.

Clark comes forward and latches onto her forearms.

"Oh doctor," Dara purrs.

Meyers is still at her back and isn't looking at anything but the cunt I just greased.

Clearing his throat twice he answers her, "Yes, Ms. Nichols."

"I demand that my examination continue. And Zoe must participate. She has a stake in this, after all." Dara's dark chuckle is muffled.

Now is the time to speak up. To tell Zo I'm sorry I fucked her friend and she can do these other guys.

Get on with her lifestyle.

But I don't.

Meyers sinks to his knees behind Dara. The dude is going to enjoy some cream pie.

Grasping her ass cheeks, he roughly spreads her and Dara leans forward, Clark accepting her weight and groans as Meyers starts to lick the dried cum from her well-used parts.

"God..." Zoe says, "That's hot-as-fuck."

Brokston turns her to face him. "Dara asked that we examine you as well." His dark eyebrows hike over midnight blue eyes.

Dara's groans grow louder as Meyers starts ramming his tongue inside her pussy.

Not to be left out, Clark takes his pants down one-handed and releases his prick from scrub prison.

As soon as his cock is free, Dara grasps his hips and begins plunging her mouth down his length.

Looking down at his own dick, Darrell notices it's standing at stiff attention. *There's something so fucking hot about a girl getting two-timed.*

Just as the thought forms, Meyers stands and lining up his prick with Dara's drenched hole, begins to push his way inside with all the delicacy of a Mac truck.

Darrell's hand goes to his cock as he begins to work his junk.

Zoe leaves Brokston's side and comes to stand before him.

I want to do what's getting done to Dara—to Zoe... but will she let him?

9

Z~

BLACK STALLION. YUM, Zoe loves Dara's coined term for her man. That is, if Darrell still is her man.

Zoe's eyes shift to Dara.

Meyers is sliding in and out of her pussy. With deft fingers, he cards her long red hair and with an expert twist, he fists the locks, pounding her from behind.

Dara's gurgled reply can't be understood because she's driving her mouth to the base of Clark's cock.

The visual leaves Zoe wet *and* sexually frustrated.

"You're just going to jack off and leave me with a case of blue clit?" Zoe accuses Darrell.

His hand slams down to the root and back up as he grunts a non-verbal.

That's just rude, though she admits Darrell's rough caress of his own cock is hot as fuck.

Zoe's fingers go to her pussy and she spreads her labia in preparation for getting off.

Dara's over there getting pounded—Zoe deserves an exam, *goddammit*. Her eyes scan the fun. Fuck *this*, if she can't have any dick, she'll play with herself.

Darrell comes forward and taking his hand off his erect cock he bats her fingers away.

"What the fuck?" *How dare he?*

"No, no—this won't do," Brokston says, his words shattering their clashed eye contact.

It's as though Darrell is teasing her, his big ten inch cock hard and ready, her sopping wet pussy that's aching to be filled.

Jerk.

Brokston cocks an eyebrow at Darrell, noting his ever-speeding hand. "He looks occupied."

He can play with himself. Oh yeah—that's fair.

Zoe notices that Darrell has one eye on Dara getting reamed by the flesh hose on both ends and one eye on her.

Fuck him. He can jack-off at the view.

Zoe's gonna *be* the view.

"He does look busy," she admits in a sarcastic tone.

"Why don't I give you an exam *and* make a deposit? Something to immunize you from germs."

Zoe knows that means and her heartbeats begin to gallop.

"Now, to execute the exam properly, I will need you to place your forehead on the floor and put your rear up as high as it will go."

Shooting Darrell a dirty look Zoe sinks to her knees and gingerly spreading her legs wide, she turns her head, placing her face on the unforgiving tile floor and hikes her hips up as she presses her forearms to the cool tile.

Zoe listens to Brokston position himself and the lightest tough of something wet and hot begins at her labia and she sighs.

Now... being eaten out she could get used to.

Dara moans and Zoe smiles, thinking they'll both be getting an "exam."

Finally.

When Dara's spiked heels appear in Zoe's line of sight Dara says, "I need you to verify that I have the right immunization."

Gulping, Zoe feels that heated slippery tongue press inside her entrance and begin a gentle in and out.

"Oh God," Zoe groans as Brokston lathes each side of her labia, stabbing her clit with the flat of his tongue he then shoots the wet organ deep inside.

Dara sinks to her haunches, gently positioning herself on the ground and widens her legs. She threads her fingers through Zoe's wet locks and lifting her head plants Zoe's mouth right on her drenched cunt.

Zoe loves cleaning and begins to lick all the delicious cum Clark and Meyers deposited.

Cream pie never tasted so good.

Where's Darrell? She takes time to wonder but can't do much because at that precise moment the tongue is gone and the solid girth of a cock starts to press inside Zoe.

She tries to turn to see what man has penetrated her but Dara admonishes, "Keep up your immunization, Zoe." She keeps Zoe's face mashed against Dara's delicious pussy.

Zoe devours Dara's juices, greedily licking and mopping up the yummy boy seed deposited just moment's before by Meyers and Clark.

"I don't think a single exam will work here," Brokston murmurs from behind Zoe as he pierces her wet twat.

"Definitely not," Darrell agrees.

Before Zoe can do anything, her legs are ruthlessly spread almost to the point of pain and where the first cock was, a second begins to slide in beside it.

"No!" Zoe cries against Dara's pussy, "I can't take two," she moans as the second big prick begins to seat itself astride the other.

"Oh yes you can!" Dara cries enthusiastically, keeping her palm pressed to the back of Zoe's skull, "Double exam time for you, naughty girl."

"I want in that cunt," Meyers or Clark says.

"Wait your exam turn," Brokston says, voice breathy.

Then the two cocks surge forward, bottoming out in her stretched-to-the-max cunt.

Zoe groans as they begin to pull out, only to rock forward inside her.

Meyers walks around and Zoe's an audience as he pulls his cock, trying to get it up again.

Apparently, the visual of her pussy being used by two pricks is making that a reality because his erection begins to go full-tilt as he walks to Dara's supine position.

Zoe comes up for air just as Meyers lowers himself to the ground above Dara's face.

He grins and without hesitation does a few hard pumps of his cock and bracing himself on either side of Dara's head he touches the tip of his prick to her lips.

Dara opens her mouth.

Plunging forward, he gags Dara with his cock, slowly fucking her mouth as Zoe's face is continuously slammed into Dara's pussy by the dual-cock fucking Zoe's getting.

A finger begins working Zoe's clit and her legs loosen as Zoe gets bitch split by the guys' rhythm.

"Ah!" Zoe wails as they give an especially deep thrust.

The finger becomes a tongue and the next sink of dicks sends her teetering over the edge.

"I'm coming," she hollers as her pussy gives deep pulses

around the dual-implanted pricks, her eyes flutter shut and her toes curl.

Zoe's eyes snap open just in time to catch Meyers stiffen above Dara as her throat works to convulsively swallow as the dicks mine Zoe's pussy trench, growing impossibly more hard then bathing her inside with cum.

The men hold her open, forcing her pussy to accept every, last drop. Zoe has no choice but to remain wide open for their use.

"That was nice," Dara says after Meyers withdraws from her mouth.

Her small, pink tongue whips out, licking up dribbling cum from the corners. "Yummy," Dara murmurs.

Zoe gives a shaky sigh as the cocks finally withdraw and she puts her weary forehead to the ground. "Oh my God." Zoe doesn't move but remains wide open.

She hardly feels it when Clark moves out from underneath her and gets into position behind her twice-deposited, dripping cunt. "I need to finish this exam," he announces.

Then his erection is slamming home in her open, lubed donut hole.

"Ah," Zoe says, thrusting backward as he rocks deeply inside. She's all loose and soaked after the double-dipping and has forgiven Darrell his insult of fucking Dara.

Because Zoe gets to fuck other men again. If she can have *her* fun—he can too.

Clark keeps up the pace and finally stiffening he keeps his prick tight and high, unloading his doctor's seed to the hilt.

Zoe wiggles her hips, trying to get all the cum in her slutty hole.

"That's not the end of this exam," Meyers reprimands

Clark, and she feels his spent cock slip out and Clark is shoved out of the way.

"Hey jackass!"

"I'm having this sloppy pussy—this last exam will commence."

Meyers is somehow hard again and begins to ram her cunt like he'll get through the other side.

But Zoe's had three cocks already and the same in cum. The warm seed sticks to the insides of the thighs as Meyers pounds her.

"Oh I love what you're doing," Dara squeals and gets to her hands and knees, reaching behind where Meyers pounds Zoe, she removes something just outside his vision.

She drags the object around where Zoe can see but Meyers cannot, wagging it slightly with a slim hand.

It's an ginormous dong—a foot? Maybe the size of a guy's wrist. *Holy fuckstick*—not like anything Zoe has seen before.

Dara pours lube over the end and with a sly wink, makes her way behind Meyers, who has his hands latched onto Zoe's hips, burying and withdrawing his cock in rapid sweeps of flesh as she grunts from his rut.

She wouldn't dare shove the thing up Meyers's ass.

Then Zoe gives the idea more thought.

Dara *might*.

After all, Zoe thinks while her body sways forward from the pounding, Dara will do *anything*.

She has.

10
D~

DARRELL LOVED DIVING into his woman again. Even though he had shlong for company.

Him and Brokston are sitting on their asses, backs against the cool tile wall as the hot water from the shower makes a soft patter against the tile floor. Their cocks are spent, slimy with Zoe's used cunt juices and other guys' jizm.

Makes Darrell want to go again. But even he can't get it up five minutes after he just fucked.

Then again, Dara's involved.

A naked Dara makes her way around Meyer's enthusiastic pumping of Zoe. Scarlet heels clickity-clack on the tile as she positions herself between him and Brokston and behind Meyers.

Meyers is really laying the pipe.

Clark stands in front of Zoe, jacking off as he watches the live action.

Zoe's legs are doing the splits while he pounds away.

That's about the time Darrell takes in the foot long dong in Dara's hand.

It's not one of those flimsy fuckers, either. It's a stiff-sized, I-mean-business, rubber whammy.

Darrell decides he's gonna enjoy the view even more.

Dara has just poured lube over the dong and turning, begins to tease Meyers' assbud on one of his withdrawals from plummeting Zo's pussy.

Dara's never been into asking for permission and starts reefing the tip inside his ass crack.

"Hey!" Meyers protests.

"Tsk-tsk," Dara says in her smooth contralto, "you don't get to grab *all* the fun."

"That's an elephant dong!" he yells.

"Technically, no," Dara says, pouring more lube on the unburied half and sliding it in another tough-won inch.

"Dara!" Zoe cries with a quick glance over her shoulder, "Ream him like he's reaming me."

"I'd be delighted," Dara replies instantly.

This'll get interesting.

Dara maneuvers her body until she's holding the dong with both hands and is dead-center behind Meyers' pumping ass.

Her legs are planted wide for stability as she plunges the dong in and out of Meyer's jettisoning hips. She digs in with gusto, pushing every time Meyer's directly plows Zoe's pussy. "Just about there," she says, pouring lube on with her right hand and pumping with her left.

"Ah!" Meyers says, "that's too much dick for me," he groans as Dara plunders his tight ass with the huge cock.

"There!" Dara announces triumphantly as she manages to plug the last, hot slippery bit to the root inside Meyers.

Brokston taps Darrell's leg and they sight in on Dara's cunt as she keeps sawing the fake dick back and forth inside Meyers.

She's completely focused on shoving that thing as far as it'll go inside Meyers and Darrell notes that only the fake nuts show.

"There we are," Dara says, driving the length home with both hands now.

"Fuck me, that feels hot," Meyers says, opening his ass to take the entire foot-long length.

Darrell's eyes widen at the sight of Meyers' asshole eating that big dick.

Brokston grins and catches Clark's eyes with a significant look... that doesn't include Darrell. Darrell's done enough fuckathons he speculates what the boys might have in store.

Clark moves around behind Dara and begins floating his large hands over the naked globes of her ass and Dara leans her head back so it rests on his shoulder but doesn't disrupt her savage pumping of Meyers.

Meyers cries out with an especially vicious plunge from Dara. She smirks and confesses, "I'm being naughty."

"You are?" Clark asks, sounding genuinely surprised.

Darrell's not. Naughty is Dara's middle name. She'll give as good as she gets.

Darrell heaves himself to his feet and Brokston joins him.

Dara turns her attention to him, green eyes blazing. "He's also been naughty; not allowing Zoe to have proper exams and immunization against the nasty little bugs one can acquire when traveling abroad." She flutters ginger eyelashes and invokes a subtle pout, ramming the dong home again.

The male pair turn their attention at Darrell, nailing him with a contemplative stare.

Darrell backs away, palms up, keenly aware of his nakedness.

Dara grins within the circle of Clark's arms as Meyers gives a mighty heave, dong embedded inside his ass and a happy Dara checking out Darrell's handy retreat.

Her hand falls away from the implanted dong as she gives Darrell her undivided attention.

"It's okay now that Zoe wants to screw other dudes. I'm on board." Darrell nods enthusiastically.

"No he's not!" Zoe accuses from the ground.

Darrell's eyes go to where she lies on her side, one leg straight and her other bent at the knee, wet hair plastered to her head, well-used pussy flaming-ass rosy pink.

Way to throw me under the bus, Zo.

"Darrell is just saying that *now*, but when we leave it's gonna be, 'Zoe you promised—Zoe I was good.'"

Her eyes gleam.

Darrell knows Zoe well enough to understand she's probably forgiven him, but she can be a sexual sadist around the edges and enjoys watching Darrell partake in things that would normally never be on his radar.

Brokston, Meyers and Clark step away from Dara. But make not mistake, Dara's the ringleader, always has been.

"Now Darrell, there's nowhere you need to be but right here with our little Internist group."

The docs murmur their assent.

She walks toward him and Darrell is helpless not to zero in on her raw-looking pussy lips. She's not gone for the hardwood floors look. Not Dara. She's ain't gonna be bald when she can flaunt a flaming red landing strip to mark the spot.

Her hips sway at her skyscraper-heeled approach.

Darrell's Adam's apple does a hard plow. "I've done enough fucking, Dara."

Her dark copper brows pull together. "I'm sorry, I thought that you came to see Zoe because you wanted an exam and vaccination as well."

Darrell blinks. *Fuck, I'm in way over my head.*

Both of them.

Dara comes to stand before him and winds her slim arms around his thick neck, pressing her soft perky breasts against his bare chest. "You be a good boy and I'll let the men use lube. Or you be a bad, bad, boy and you get what you get."

Darrell doesn't think long on it. "Lube."

"That's right. You be a good *patient*," Dara enunciates the last word with a meat cleaver, "and let the good doctors use their tools on you."

Clark moves to her side, Brokston and Meyers flanking the other.

"Don't know if I have enough immunization... fluid," Clark admits.

Dara grabs his nutsack, lightly squeezing. "What?" she cocks her head to the side, crimson brow arched, green gaze razoring down on his face.

Clark rises to his tiptoes. "Maybe wrong there, Ms. Nichols."

"I *thought* I misheard you," she murmurs then turns her attention to Brokston and Meyers.

Meyers puts up a hand with a soft chuckle. "We're good."

"The blue pill is a wonder drug," Brokston elaborates.

She releases Clark's balls and his exhale is pure relief. Her dubious expression turns on the others. "Yes—" Dara's eyes run down the length of the naked men. "—but can you produce sufficient immunization?"

"I think they'll have to prove that," Zoe says from her elbow and Darrell startles at her presence.

Her sly smile takes in his expression.

"Hands and knees, baby—it's time you became a more active participate in our exam. I've been thoroughly examined and found to be..." Zoe directs the question at the three doctors.

Clark shrugs. "Perfect."

Brokston's blue eyes twinkle, "Wet and ready."

Dara frowns and he corrects, "Ready for travel, Ms. Nichols."

"All the necessary protocol is in place for Ms. Scott; she is cleared for all activities," Meyers states.

Dara turns a beaming smile on Meyers. "Since your answer was the most well-though out, you may administer the first exam on Darrell."

Darrell opens his mouth to speak his piece.

Dara presses her fingers to his lips.

Zoe bends underneath Dara's outstretched arm and he's suddenly looking into big brown eyes he knows so well.

"Be a good boy and take your medicine, Darrell. Like I did mine."

Darrell deliberates for a sec then finally shrugs his shoulders. How hard can it be? Zoe fucked all those guys in a row and she's still running around.

"I guess I can use an... exam," he reluctantly admits as he walks around the ground and over to the shower spray. He backs up into the water, letting the heated water settle his nerves.

It's been awhile since he did a train, and he's still not sure how he felt about getting plugged from both ends.

Darrell's not even sure if that's going to be what happens.

When Zoe walks to the opposite shower and starts sudsing off the dong that Meyers got shoved deep in his ass, Darrell begins to imagine he knows what the plan will be—in part.

Darrell's all about the girls and has just let men fuck him because Zoe was involved.

But speculating about that huge dildo crammed up his ass—with plenty of lube—make his dick start to get hard.

And when Brokston sinks to his knees in front of Darrell? God help him, he guides the other dude's head right to his cock, where Brokston's blue eyes meet his for a split second, right before making a tight wet seal with his lips.

ORAL EXAM
A Dara Nichols World Novelette
Volume 5

New York Times BESTSELLER
MARATA EROS

Copyright © 2021 by Marata Eros
All rights reserved.
No part of this book may be reproduced in any form or by any electronic or mechanical means, including information storage and retrieval systems, without written permission from the author, except for the use of brief quotations in a book review.

11

D~

BROKSTON DOESN'T FUCK off—taking his time with dick-sucking.

Nope.

The other man makes a tight seal on the tip of Darrell's hard cock and drives his mouth to the base like a locomotive, struggling to take the entire length.

Failing, Brokston begins to gag.

Darrell loves the noises Brokston makes and holds his head there at the base even as the dude begins to struggle.

His eyes lift at the sound of Dara's heels strike the hard tile as she moves around them, her hand gripping something he can't make out in his periphery.

Darrell feels a whip-like sting as Dara strikes his ass with something smooth and hard. *What the...?* Darrell startles and surprised, he releases Brokston's dark head.

The dude comes up for air, sputtering, blue eyes flashing on Darrell's face.

The sound of whistling fills the air a second time.

Crack! His ass cheeks bunch, hips thrusting forward. The

strike burns like a lash of fire. "Shee-it, girl! *Damn* with that fucking thing."

Darrell begins to turn around but is shoved roughly from behind.

Zoe's sexy laugh sounds from his left.

"My turn!" Brokston says as firm hands grab Darrell's shoulders from behind, pushing him forward.

Darrell automatically folds at the waist and Brokston guides his head to his substantial cock.

Turnaround is fair play. Darrell likes to get *sucked* –but isn't always into *doing it*.

Today doesn't seem to be about *his* needs, however.

"Suck it! Suck it!" Zo twitters from behind him, the sound of her clapping her hands in glee loud in the echo-y locker room.

Darrell opens wide and begins going down on Brokston. When he gets Brokston nice and lubed, Darrell adds a hand, stroking up and down just ahead of his lips.

Brokston takes full advantage of Darrell's hot wet mouth, and shoves Darrell's soaked seal all the way down to the root.

Darrell gags—he's used to eating pussy, not pole. His natural urge is to fight for air and his arms begin to flail.

Meyers and Clark each grab an arm as Darrell's butt cheeks are spread by feminine hands.

"Just like that, yeah," Zoe instructs and Dara adds, "I'm going to make a bullseye of his lovely stallion trench."

Darrell makes headway getting off Brokston's dick but then Dara begins to plant the tip of the huge dong in Darrell's assbud.

At least, Darrell *thinks* it's the dildo.

When large hands peg his hips—Darrell knows better. His eyes widen at the familiar sensation.

"Yeah, man, stuff it in there!"

Meyers.

Cold liquid flows over the top of his ass and onto the stiff cock working its way deep inside Darrell's crack.

Darrell begins enjoying the sensation of blowing Brokston as one of the two doctors plummet his ass.

"Man his ass is tight," Meyers says in a reedy voice.

Zoe giggles. "He doesn't get the beef fuel injection enough. And he *definitely* doesn't want his immunization."

The rocking inside him slows. "He doesn't?" Meyers says as Darrell feels his throbbing cock finally bottom out in his lubed asshole.

"No," Dara murmurs with obvious humor threading through the one-word answer.

"We'll take care of that," Meyers says as he resumes going to town on Darrell's ass again.

Meanwhile, Clark walks around and placing his hand on the back of Darrell's head, presses his face onto Brokston's cock.

Brokston gives a pleased grunt at the new rhythm. "Keep that up, Clark—I got a *lot* of immunization to give this patient."

Darrell can't help the groan that escapes his lips as Meyers begins to pack his ass with his prick, jamming the spear of flesh hard and high over and over.

Darrell's cock helplessly hardens as he sights Clark begin to lower himself at eye level where Darrell's engorged dick hangs between his swollen nuts.

Brokston takes over, carding fingers through Darrell's short, tight curls and rapidly moves his head up and down his soaked crank.

Darrell's hand cups the other dude's balls and Brokston

groans in pleasure just as Clark does the same to Darrell's cock and balls.

Fuck that feels good. Darrell moans from the handling of his filled balls.

"Gonna come," Brokston announces in a breathy whisper, driving his dick down Darrell's throat.

Hot. Darrell starts to involuntarily drive his hips forward, unable to stop while he's sucking cock and getting his asshole reamed.

Clark latches onto Darrell's rigid dick and he moans around Brokston's cock.

Darrell needed this action.

Suddenly Brokston's cock grows impossibly harder and his dick begins to unload hot cum directly into Darrell's mouth.

Darrell gulps the thick load down as Brokston holds his head against his dick.

Meyers continues to drive his hips forward then abruptly stops, planted high and deep within Darrell's ass trench.

The sensation of warmth spreads deep inside him when Clark's mouth touches the tip of Darrell's dick he knows he won't be able to hold back for long with a dick in each hole and a dude sucking his cock.

When Darrell ass cheeks get spread further, a soft, spent cock withdraws and a stiff, huge one put in its place.

The dildo.

None too gently one of the girls starts to beef the huge thing in his ass and Clark's hands grip Darrell's ass, spreading his cheeks wider as his mouth continues its tight wet rhythm up and down the length of Darrell's cock.

In and out one of the women plunges the dildo as Clark

makes short work of Darrell's prick, driving up and down the hard rod of flesh.

The pressure in his nuts builds until he finally tips over the edge. "AH!" Darrell's hoarse shout echoes in the locker room as he comes from his toes.

Clark sucks him down, still gently pumping his softening dick to get every last, hot drop.

Exhausted, Darrell begins to slump to his knees, Brokston cock flopping out of his mouth.

"Oh no, baby—you don't get to rest on the job."

Darrell's eyes widen.

Zoe's eyes glitter from where she's laid down on the tile. Spreading her legs she points to her bright pink hole and whispers, "Put your cum-tongue right here."

By simple deduction, Darrell realizes it's Dara that keeps re-lubing the dildo and pumping it in his ass.

The sensation of the huge dong makes his spend dick twitch in anticipation.

Maybe he *can* get it up that fast.

His eyes move to Zoe's pussy as he thinks of all the things he can do to her cunt.

Cum dribbles out of his mouth.

Fuck it.

Darrell gives in, lowering his upper body down by his elbows as he centers himself between her spread legs and readies his mouth.

His cock is already halfway-to-hard just thinking about stabbing his cum-drenched tongue deep inside his women's hole while Dara corkscrews his ass with a dick too big for his ass to take.

12

Z~

ZOE'S CAGED HER man good this time.

Her eyes meet Dara's from over her Darrell as he stabs his tongue deep in her wet hole.

Just thinking about the cum getting inserted in her drenched twat has Zoe spreading her legs further apart. That, and the rhythm of the dong Dara keeps shoving in his hole.

Unbelievably, Darrell is hard again and after he makes her wet with all the tongue thrusting he comes up for air, his body gently rocking with the dong pounding in his ass.

"Fuck me, Darrell," Zoe commands.

Dark eyes flashing within a determined face, Darrell instructs, "Turn around—hands and knees."

Zoe grins—she knows *this* game.

He pushes up and Zoe notices he doesn't ask Dara to stop his ass-fucking. If anything, Darrell spreads his knees even wider to take the huge dildo as deep as the big plug can be planted.

Zoe hurries to close her legs and turn, sending her ass-end high in the air.

She knows from intimate experience taking a cock as big as Darrell's will spread her wide and she can't wait for that exquisite stretch. And the fact that he's probably frustrated over how he ended up here, on the locker room floor, getting ass-fucked and sucking dick should make the pounding that much sweeter.

Darrell should understand by now if he wants to play with Zoe in her sexual sandbox, things will get saucy and sexual encounters will be mixed, unpredictable and hot-as-fuck.

Large hands cover the globes of her ass and grip, fingertips biting into her soft, round cheeks.

Zoe groans, placing her forehead against the cool tile, prepared to be plundered.

"Nope, this is double-duty time," one of the three interns says.

Zoe looks up as Brokston softly strikes her face with the tip of his dick.

He's hanging, awkwardly suspended above her face and she licks the tip of his smooth, swollen head and the stiff rod of flesh reactively twitches.

"Ram it!" one of the others calls out.

Dara's mad giggle sounds. "I am *definitely* ramming it," Zoe hears Dara announce lightly.

"No, Ms. Nichols, I'm addressing Brokston."

Oh.

"Well it works nicely for both pursuits, doesn't it, Doctor?" Dara's coy lilt replies.

A grunt of assent sounds.

When Zoe's hair is fisted by Brokston, her scalp tingles as Brokston's little blue pill magic has taken affect and his dirty rod, covered in cum and yummy boy saliva parts her full lips for entry.

With a moan Zoe acquiescences, mowing down to the base in one smooth motion. Brokston holds her head at the root and she begins to thrash from the extreme length and breadth of his hard cock.

Not breathing is part of the excitement and Brokston seems to realize that little fact, letting Zoe off his cock *just* long enough to suck an inhale then slamming her lips to the root of his prick again.

Brokston's head falls back and he grunts as he begins the slow fucking of her mouth.

Zoe's pussy moistens and Darrell begins to tease her opening with his smooth, mushroom-shaped head as her head bobs with Brokston's deep prick insertion then releases with a pop to steal another breath before he drives her back down.

"Ah!" Zoe shouts around his wet dick as Darrell begins shoving each, hard-won inch inside her pussy.

"That's right," Dara says, "I want Zoe to be *thoroughly examined* and if Darrell needs to be an assistant—the more the merrier."

Zoe's getting hotter, especially with Dara's naughty words in the background.

"I think we have one more thing that must be accomplished," Dara announces.

Zoe feels the cool slide of a thick gel being used above her ass bud just as Darrell gains the last bit of her twat and bottoms out, throbbing inside her.

Zoe's mouth isn't free to protest even is she wanted to as her ass cheeks are spread by the familiar touch of Darrell's hands.

Dara begins to sink her finger inside Zoe's assbud and she squirms under the onslaught of Darrell banging deep and taking Brokston inside her mouth all the way.

Dara's light insistent touch plugs her reluctant ass then starts a slow, teasing pump of her finger.

Zoe loves getting all her holes filled but with how big the dudes' cocks are she has all she can take.

"My patient needs a more vigorous probe than *that*." Zoe recognizes Clark's voice.

Suddenly, Dara's finger withdraws and a huge something begins poking her rear entry.

Zoe's pretty sure she can't take the dildo that's gotten shoved in everyone's holes and moves to evade the huge cock by squeezing her ass cheeks together.

"No ya don't, Zo," Darrell rumbles from behind her, "you *take* your medicine.

Then her ass is spread, totally vulnerable to whatever Clark wants to put inside and Zoe feels the gradual insertion of the hugest dildo she's ever taken.

Zoe's pussy gets wetter and Darrell begins to pound her hard, her body rocking back and forward with the rough treatment as the motion forces her head down even further on Brokston's cock.

"No!" she gasps as her mouth clears the end of Brokston's cock.

"Yes, you *take* your medicine," Clark says in a satisfied tone and the huge dildo begins to pry her ass apart to epic proportions.

Darrell piston-drives his cock deep as Clark wiggles the dildo in until the massive length is seated about halfway.

Zoe's holes are filled and she's sure she'll split, when Clark manages to get the dildo all the way, Zoe's too plugged to move.

But the men take over, Brokston slams her head to the base of his cock as Darrell drives his big prick to the end of her.

Clark begins the slow ass-fucking with the dildo and Zoe's lost, unable to get away from the three-way cock-stabbing.

She's a slut and spreads her legs, taking both huge cocks in her plugged wet holes and the one inside her mouth, groaning, she gets owned by all three at the same time.

Dara sinks to her hands and knees, shimming underneath Zoe's body and when she is eye-level to Zoe's pussy she begins to lick and suck Zoe's clit.

"Oh my God!" Zoe cries as she lifts from Brokston's crank just as he guides her mouth back to the tip of his dick and says, "Swallow your medicine."

He pushes her head down and she takes his dick inside her mouth, his cum spurting out the tip endlessly.

Zoe loves playing the whore throat convulsing as she drinks all the yummy boy juice down.

Dara relentlessly flicks her tongue back and forth on Zoe's clit, ruthlessly lashing the tender bundle of nerves.

Darrell plants his prick and as she feels it harden, Clark begins to assault her ass like she's a whore.

Zoe begins to helplessly come around Darrell's big cock. Pussy pulsing, Clark drives the dong deep in her ass as she comes.

Darrell withdraws with a grunt but they're not done with her slutty pussy.

Someone gets in behind and begins fucking her lubed cunt, pounding her from behind.

After a few deep thrusts Meyer's shouts, "Coming," and plants his prick deep.

He withdraws and cum begins to run down the inside of her leg as Zoe watches Clark's legs walk to stand behind her.

Before he takes his turn he shoves the huge dildo in her

ass over and over again, clearly enjoying using the huge toy on her ass.

Then his dick is sliding in her loose hole.

"Oh this is nice... so wet, still tight enough to come in," he whispers and begins his pounding.

Zoe loves to be filled to overflowing with different men's loads and spreads her legs as wide as they will go without falling.

Her pussy is getting filled and Dara has squeezed out from underneath her and taken the back door position of shoving the dildo in her ass bud to the end.

"Coming," Clark whispers as he fills her pussy to the brim with his load.

Her pussy is so full of cum now that it can't hold the load and exhausted and with three loads of cum slipping out from her saturated hole, Zoe lays her head against the tile just as one of the interns says, "There's more medicine for Ms. Scott to receive."

Zoe looks up just as the locker room door opens and more men begin walking into the locker room.

13

Z~

ZOE'S NOT GONNA lie; things look serious when ten guys pile into the locker room.

"Oh goody," Dara says from underneath Zoe.

Goody?

Dara scoots out from beneath Zoe and her next exhale is a shaky breath of pure excitement.

"This is fantastic," Brokston says thoughtfully, walking toward the newcomers and nodding his head enthusiastically. "I mean, we could use *more* examiners."

What? Zoe looks between the original trio and Dara, then the new guys.

"Exactly my thoughts," Dara chimes in.

Fuck *this*. Zoe's been the one getting taken, now she wants to do some taking of her own.

Zoe gets to her feet just as the last dude walks through the door and pressing the flat of his palms to the surface, shoves it closed and throws the latch.

Ten pairs of eyes stare at Zoe.

She supposes it's worth a look. Being as how Zoe's

standing there without a stitch of clothing on and cum running down the inside of her legs.

Of course, that last part is all well-and-good.

Darrell comes to stand by her side and she gives him a side look. "We good?" Zoe crosses her arms beneath her large boobs.

He nods. "I dig this is what you want, Zo."

"Pfft," she smacks his bicep, "After all the dick you've taken, it seems to me that it's what *you* want too."

Darrell pulls an irritated face and she swings a palm out, the gesture silently saying: *refute the logic*.

He can't, is what. Darrell's as into this as her and Dara.

Dara strides by Darrell and flogs him with the dong as she passes. "Yes, what dear Zoe said," she quips, heels still attached as she walks over to the new "examiners."

"My pussy, my choice," Dara says as they line up she pivots, directing her next question at the three docs, Brokston, Clark and Meyers. "Are you sure these *examiners* are qualified?"

Brokston shrugs. "They came highly qualified."

Meyers chortles behind him.

"I believe that it is Ms. Nichols who needs the most thorough exam as she's scheduled to travel before Ms. Scott." Clark spreads his arms away from his body as though this is the most matter-of-fact pronouncement ever made.

"Not unless my man and I," Zoe jerks a thumb in Darrell's direction, "can have equal treatment."

Dara's lower lip pouts, her green eyes scraping over Zoe. "Well, now, I've been *very* generous with my attentions, dearest Zoe."

True. But Zoe wants to be tag-teamed just as much as Dara. Zoe ruminates on that. Maybe not *quite* as much.

She smirks, back-pedaling. "I'm not saying you *haven't*

worked me over just like I like—I just want to be a part of the *new* action."

"Oh you will be," Dara says, dismissing Zoe as she turns around, and giving the weight of her gaze to the ten men.

Zoe takes time to inventory the dudes then frowns. Right away she sees a massive problem.

Clothes.

Apparently, Dara sorts the same thing in short order, waving a slim palm around in their general direction. "Off with the Doctor smocks."

One especially tall and well-built stud starts to comment on how *he* likes things.

Dara steps forward with the dong still in hand and grabs his nuts with her free hand, giving it a gentle squeeze.

His eyes tighten.

Maybe not so gentle, Zoe deliberates.

"Though I appreciate your perspective, things will actually be my way," Dara restates for the uninitiated.

Their eyes meet.

"Are we clear, Doctor...?"

"Talbot," he manages, starting to rise on his tiptoes.

"Excellent, Doctor Talbot," she says crisply. "Shall we begin with you?" Dara's eyes gleam.

She does like to break the men who show resistance.

Zoe likes a compliant male and she knows that Dara absolutely does.

Taking Darrell's hand Zoe tugs him over to the line-up then looks over her shoulder at the three docs. "I guess this is goodbye."

Brokston's dark blue eyes widen. "But—"

"Nope," Zoe softly cuts him off, "You've done your exam on Dara and me—*and* Darrell," she emphasizes, "now let your colleagues have a turn."

"No, Zoe—let the good doctors stay to supervise." Dara admonishes.

Zoe rakes her eyes over the doctors' used, soft dicks. "If they stay, they play," she states.

"But of course," Dara agrees, arching a dark ginger brow above one of her brilliant green eyes.

"We can get our tools ready," Clark says indignantly.

Zoe giggles.

She's loving the script and the way Dara herds the men like feral cats into her erotic design.

Loves it.

"I don't know if my ass crack can take much more fuckery," Darrell admits.

Dara of the sharp hearing says, "Your ass crack will take what we give it."

Zoe flicks her eyes to his impressive junk and notices he's already semi-hard again, deciding Darrell kinda likes the passive-aggressive vibe of reluctance that's been a theme for today.

Truth is, her black stallion likes other stallions *just fine*.

"All right," Dara mutters, deep in thought as the men begin to disrobe. "Eeeny-meeny miney moe," she chimes as her long legs strut down the row of neatly lined-up men.

Now that's *diversity,* Zoe thinks. Fuck race. *Just give me an entire buffet of penises to choose from and I'll choke on all that glorious cum.*

Dara goes back to Talbot (who's now conveniently naked) and bending at the waist, she takes his cock in her mouth. "Hmmm," she moans, doubling down on his erection, she begins a smooth practiced seesaw, giving his stiff prick hard, wet attention.

"Wow," Talbot says, throwing his head back, "This is a fine start to our oral exam."

Dara pops her lips off, straightening.

"What?" Talbot asks, eyes already going glassy.

She puts her manicured fingertip to his lips. "Quiet, I am the patient and I do the talking, but first," Dara expertly turns on her stiletto heels and clicks back to where Clark, Meyers and Brokston stand, flopping the huge, used dong at Brokston's feet. "Clean that instrument thoroughly," she cackles, "and be careful when you pick up the soap."

"Yes, Ms. Nichols. Whatever we have to do to put your mind at ease," Clark adds quickly.

Meyers and the other two move to where the shower spray runs endlessly and begin to soap the gigantic dildo.

Dara turns, giving Zoe a triumphant look as she walks past her and Darrell.

Zoe grins. No one can refute that Dara is the master sexual planner.

Or mistress.

"Now, where were we?" she muses, tapping her chin with a scalding hot red nail. "Ah yes. First, we," she inclines her head in Zoe's direction, "will need a thorough clean and prep between exams."

"Yes," Talbot and the other doctors chorus in unison.

Perfect.

"Come along," Dara says and Zoe takes in the train of men, pricks bobbing as they walk toward the communal showers.

Dara kicks off her crimson heels before she enters the tiled floor and the spray of steaming water jettisons her from all sides.

She lifts her arms like a jeanie, swaying beneath the spray.

"Come clean me," Dara announces.

"Who?" Talbot asks, brows together, eyes moving to the men and clearly indicating *which one?*

Her green eyes flash back at him. "All of you, of course."

Zoe catches the three doctors smirk knowingly and Dara gives them a sharp look of reprimand, missing nothing.

"You three, are you quite done with sterilizing the instrument of examination?"

"Ah-*um*... yes," Meyers stutters.

"Then run over here and take care of me. After all, you insisted you could still perform an examination if Zoe and I allowed you to stay."

Zoe likes being looped.

Dara's eyes stray to a silent Darrell and she flutters her fingers at him. "And Darrell."

Looped her stallion, too.

Darrell and Zoe walk to the showers.

"If you, ah—bend over," Talbot suggests in a slightly hoarse voice, "I think I can reach all the difficult-to-clean parts."

Dara's sultry chuckle echoes in the strange acoustics of the locker room.

"Sure. Just let me see if I can still touch... my toes."

As promised Dara bends over in half, easily touching her toes. Zoe admires her fine slitted bare cunt, water rinsing away the cum from their fun.

Talbot takes a shaky breath, obviously loving the same view as Zoe then reaches out to the soap holder and grabs the bar, slowly lathering up his hands. When they're completely obscured by fragrant suds he turns to Zoe, his bright hazel eyes and extreme height mesmerizing her. "Why don't you and..." he looks at Darrell.

"Your other patient," Dara supplies in a muffled voice.

"Yes—our other patient," Talbot says as though in a trance, "assume the same position as Ms. Nichols?"

Zoe's not sure she's as flexible as Dara and mentions that.

Darrell echoes her.

Talbot's smile is like the Cheshire cat as he walks toward them, hands well-lubed with soap.

"That's fine, do what you can."

Zoe and Darrell bend over.

14

D~

HOLY FUCK, HE'S gonna do this. Like right now.

Darrell is excited. He's had mixed feelings before; conflicted as fuck. Because he should dig the white picket fence, the "settle down" thing that everyone else is jonesing for. Right?

But every time him and Zo get into one of Dara's sexual schemes, he starts out pissed and ends up getting off, bigtime.

What's really hot is the not *knowing*. Just pure anticipation of getting his ass rode.

"This won't do," he hears that Brokston dude say and they move Zoe just in front of him.

Darrell cranes his neck, trying to figure out what's not gonna "do."

Then he gets it.

Brokston's hands are full of suds and he begins cleaning Zoe's delicious cunt. He's not shy about it, either.

They're close to the shower head and as the water beats down on her shoulders, the rivulets travel to the small of her back then right into her hot crack.

"Cleaning her parts," Brokston says in a heated whisper.

Darrell can't help himself and bent over like he is, he doesn't have anything else to do.

He inserts a finger inside her slick hole.

Zoe moans, writhing around the digit.

Darrell begins to pump his finger in and out as Brokston strokes apart her plump pussy lips.

"That's it, clean her cunt," Brokston murmurs.

Zoe rocks back, spreading her thick thighs and Darrell loves the look of her hot pink pussy splayed open and vulnerable to whatever might need to be put inside.

Brokston finishes washing her entire drenched pussy while Darrell continues to slide his index finger in and out, faster and faster.

Brokston stands, moving away from Zoe and heading to Dara.

"Finally," she says, scorching him with her emerald gaze, "I was beginning to think your bedside manner was lacking."

"Never!" Brokston replies enthusiastically.

Darrell watches as Dara's cunt gets saturated by soap and Brokston does a jaw flick in her direction and the men move in.

He can't wait to see the girls get fucked.

When he feels his back end getting soaped Darrell relaxes for the ass-reaming he knows he'll get.

∽

Dara

THERE'S no way around it. Dara's pleasure pot is simply *juicy*. And the exams so far have been lovely, however, the procedures been lacking a bit in the thoroughness department.

What Dara needs now is *several* inoculations. One after another, after another.

Yes. Then she would be fully sated and prepared for her holiday with both Zoe and Isabella.

She determines that all these exams are critical for her well-being.

Dara makes a note that Isabella should be included in the next round of examinations. And, after their arrival to a balmy destination, there would be a need of foreign examinations as well. She believes in comprehensive "medical" treatment and receiving the proper number of exams.

Brokston strokes his fingers down Dara spine and when his hands cup her ass cheeks she says, "Now let the other doctors give me this exam. They're able to fully sanitize the area as well, Doctor."

"I'm senior here," Brokston says, attempting to unfurl his peacock feathers.

I see, Dara thinks and straightens from her fun lean.

Turning, she faces Brokston and redundantly grabs his balls as she'd done with Talbot.

"I am the patient and will be deferred to," she restates with crisp enunciation.

"Is that a question?" Brokston asks softly, while Dara literally has a hold of his nutsack.

She squeezes.

Brokston's eyes tighten.

"No. It's not a question, my reminder of deference should enlighten you about who owns the hierarchy in the room."

Dara narrows her eyes on the good doctor, who is clearly new to the situation.

And who is ultimately in charge.

"You?" Brokston guesses.

"Pfft," Dara gives a sultry growl, "Of course, *me*. Now run off and herd the men in this direction."

Dara's lips curl as Brokston doesn't waste any time, herding a small group of about five males in her direction while saving the other half for Darrell and Zoe.

Dara runs her tongue along her full lower lip, anticipating the delight of watching men getting their ass crack polished by instruments and understands that facing Darrell while *he* gets his ass fucked will add more excitement to her own exam.

She faces the group of doctors who walk toward her with a firm smile in place.

This will be fun.

Darrell and she lock eyes and Dara winks at the black stallion, noting that he stomped around at first, blustering about Zoe this and Zoe that, only to succumb to Dara's agenda, as per usual.

Two doctors position themselves behind her and Dara notices that Talbot is first in line. *Of course.*

"I have my own equipment," he announces.

"What?" Dara begins to turn to see what that equipment is but he fists her long hair, disallowing movement. "No. You're not allowed to look at what instrument I'll use," he says haughtily.

Well, well. Dara's tight cunt gets swollen with anticipation.

One of the two of them grip her hips and widening her aggressively, a hand begins to massage and thoroughly clean her parts. Spreading her labia, a finger beginning to seesaw back and forth on her plump clit.

Dara tires to wiggle but they keep her spread, ready to own her pussy in any way they want.

Darrell attempts to squirm away when hands land on his ass.

Dara watches as one of the other two doctors begins cleaning Darrell's backend of all the fun he's already had with Brokston, Meyers and Clark.

Zoe's front has been nearly been pressed to the floor again, ass-end up and is servicing Clark's cock as Meyers and Brokston jerk their junk in a loose circle around her.

Excellent, Dara thinks, not wanting to be held responsible for their instrument fail.

Sweeping her gaze over the trio's erections, she's pleased to see that *won't* be an issue.

One man kneels underneath Darrell and begins kneading his balls, stroking the soap all over the tight nutsacks, cupping his hands with water, he takes his time rinsing them off.

Dara's favorite part is when the doctor assumes a hands and knees position and softly takes one of Darrell's nuts in his mouth.

Darrell groans, parting his ass cheeks, clearly begging for a rear entry.

The doctor keeps rolling Darrell's single testicle inside his mouth and at the precise moment he switches to the other one, the doctor behind Darrell begins to insert the largest natural cock Dara has ever had the pleasure of witnessing.

The instant she takes in the length and girth of that anaconda prick, Dara wants to be fucked by it.

"Oh my God," she breathes as Darrell's ass begins to eat the tip of the thing.

The doctor who is pushing his humongous cock inside Darrell mutters, "Such a tight little hole."

"Stretch him!" Dara calls out.

Zoe grunts her agreement.

Another doctor moves in front of Darrell and using more soap, starts to stroke up and down on Darrell's cock while the other doctor sucks first one nut then the other.

Darrell calls out, begging for a break from the huge, natural flesh that continues to plunder his ass.

The corners of Dara's lips twitch. That's not the way exams work in her world.

He needs an injection.

Darrell's hips begin moving in time to the doctor who's stroking him, the soap adding a slick, non-resistant rhythm.

The doctor giving Darrell his huge dick continues to inch inside, widening Darrell's ass.

Darrell makes a sound of protest and the doctor soaping his cock pushes Darrell's head down to his own prick while continuing to jack Darrell off as he uses the spray of heated water as lubricant.

Dara watches Darrell get owned.

Finally, the huge prick is half-buried in Darrell's ass and the doctor begins the fucking, pulling the huge cock out of Darrell halfway, he plunges back in.

Darrell howls around the other doctor's cock but keeps ramming his face down the other man's erection.

They begin to fuck Darrell's ass and mouth as Darrell helplessly moves between the two, getting both his holes owned.

The doctor slamming his cock home in Darrell's mouth lets a hoarse shout go, pressing Darrell's mouth to the base of him and spasming his cum deep inside Darrell's throat.

Darrell eats the cum, swallowing the entire load down in

great gulps while the doctor ramming his elephant cock inside Darrell finally bottoms out, Darrell's ass cheeks spread completely.

Dragging the enormous erection back out, he shoves it in all the way, planting the thick prick deep and spraying his seed high.

Darrell lifts his head from the spent cock and begins to come as the last pull of his cock sends him over the edge and the doctor beneath releases his balls, placing his lips over Darrell's spurting cock and drinking him down all the way.

Every drop.

15

Z~

HER MAN IS getting an ass-reaming like never before and Zoe's jelly.

She's just getting her head shoved down on whatever doc is swinging his dick around.

Zoe likes being spread *wide*.

Her eyes challenge Dara's from across the room. Zoe wants to maneuver Dara to get that horse cock.

Dara deserves a small lesson for fucking Darrell.

Or a big one. Her lips smile around the dick she's sucking. Zoe contains her snigger—easy when she's blowing dick.

The three original docs must understand this because Clark and Meyers catch her eye and there's a twinkle in theirs.

They walk from where they'd been an avid audience to Dara getting lubed and finger-fucked to speak quietly to the guy who is owner of said horse cock.

They glance over at Dara, then at Zoe.

Nope! She thinks fiercely—Dara *first*.

The men don't have far to walk.

Darrell's ass is free of the guy's huge dick and he collapses to the ground, groaning.

Zoe keeps her head bobbing on the cock planted in her mouth and shifts gears because his rod gets harder and the dude starts coming.

Swallow or choke is *not* just a saying.

Finally, the dude is done and with a sucking gasp and gurgle, Zoe releases her relentless vacuum of his cock and he staggers back.

Big dick saunters over, all six and a half feet of sleek black thoroughbred. "You want your twat spread?" he asks in a gravely deep baritone.

Well, that's direct. Her eyes skate down to his junk.

The dude's already half-hard.

Zoe starts a slow perusal from his toes, her eyes driving up to hover over the most impressive equipment on a man she's ever seen. Gulping, she continues to his flat stomach that sports an eight-pack. Once at the pecs, her eyes roam horizontally, taking in a fine, muscled chest that's so broad she couldn't hug him.

Zoe runs the tip of her tongue over her lips.

Yum.

He is similar to Zoe's black stallion, but where that similarity starts, their likeness in looks abruptly ends with eyes that sweep in the corners to almond-shaped.

This dude is exotic.

And hung.

"I do," Zoe finally answers. She flutters her eyes, and with a casualness that comes naturally, lets her legs flop apart.

Now, the docs cleaned her and Darrell. Zoe hasn't had a fresh injection of cum since, but that doesn't mean there might be a *little* bit of the excessive loads that still want to dribble out of her cunt with gravity's assistance.

Like now.

Hot cum slithers out of her well-used but mainly clean hole and Big Dick notices the jism-slide right away, his breaths piling up one on top of the other.

Some folks just get their rocks off on cream pie. Zoe's sympathetic since cum (and lots of it) certainly gets hers off.

"Zo!" Darrell calls out, trying to sit up, but apparently, his gorgeous ass is on the sore side and he's struggling to stand.

"Busy, baby." Zoe snickers then wastes a glance on him. "Negotiating my *healthcare* here." She winks.

Darrell bites back a moan.

Zoe whips her face back to Big Dick. She's certain he has a name but how important could that be considering his unique anatomy?

Besides, she enjoys BD.

"But," she continues and with slow precision, wets the tip of her index finger and uses it to slide between her pussy lips and begin to work her own clit.

BD's gaze latches onto the movement.

"I want you to inject Dara *first*." Zoe mock-pouts, her finger getting into an excellent rhythm.

BD crosses his arms over his muscular chest, cock giving an appealing bob with the motion. "That's great but I can't fuck *everyone*."

Her eyes widen, finger flying. "Why not?"

He barks a laugh, a smile slashing white in his dark face. "'Cause, I need to rest between fucks."

Brokston, God love him, sidles up beside BD and withdraws a small, circular plastic jar from his doctor's smock.

(Zoe notes he's not wearing anything else but appreciates his stab at professionalism.)

"I have these to boost your energy level."

The long, blue pills are ones Zoe knows well.

Brokston raises the hand that holds the bottle and moves it back and forth, rattling the pills while Meyers trots up with a full glass of water.

Mr. Preparedness, Zoe thinks, panting as she breathlessly brings herself closer to a blowup orgasm.

Clark pipes in with, "Bottoms up!"

Zoe loves their enthusiasm.

BD is a team player and silently takes the pill that Brokston helpfully plucks from the holder and shoots it toward the back of his throat.

Grabbing the cup of water, he chases the pill to the end.

His chin lowers from drinking and he wipes off the excess water with the back of his hand.

"It will take a bit of time to go into effect," Clark murmurs apologetically.

BD shakes his head, eyes zeroed in on Zoe's pussy.

"Doesn't matter," his dark brown eyes take in Zoe's spread legs as just then she blows her cork with a sultry shout.

Lowering to his hands and knees, BD positions himself between her thighs, "I'll eat her until I can fuck the redhead."

Zoe is coming down from her post-orgasmic buzz, *sounds good to me*.

Leaning back, she finds there's a dude staged behind her like a handy, man-sized pillow.

Life is good.

∽

D~

Darrell's back to his nose being out of joint. That dick in his back door had been fucking hot.

The guy not only has a huge dick, but what seems to be an equal supply of cum.

Darrell outta know, all that hot seed is slipping out of his ass bud as he crawls over to his smartie pants woman.

But things are getting majorly out of control as he watches the guy who just did him, eat Zoe's twat like a buffet.

Dara's sexual soiree is epic but Darrell's too sore to stand and the girls are vulnerable to getting over-fucked.

Maybe it's time to switch out to lighter weight shit. And for once, Darrell thinks this dude's cock should not be in his woman.

He doesn't think Zoe will ever recover from that cock.

Hell—Darrell doesn't think *he* will.

Darrell scoped Brokston slipping the guy a blue pill. Viagra will pick his shit up with a stiffy that never quits.

Turning his head, he sees Dara's getting line-fucked. But what's interesting this time is she's bent over, and no one is fucking her endlessly. Instead, they're definitely doing a cum dumpster train; beat off until they're just about ready to blow then bulls eyeing their dicks at the last, possible second while off-loading their cream into her cougar cunt.

Darrell wants some of that, and finds he's already hard even after getting jacked off.

He glances at Zoe.

She's writhing on the floor as the biggest cock in the room goes to town on her twat.

"Oh yeah!" she hollers as he stabs the stout flesh sword of his tongue into her pussy.

Fuck it. Changing direction, Darrell begins to crawl toward Dara. He wants to offload too and he's still a bit pissed at Zoe.

Dara will spread her whore legs for him. He just has to manage standing to stick his dick in her.

As luck would have it, by the time he gets over there, the last doctor has slipped their used cock out of her slippery snatch.

Darrell can't make out her pussy for all the frothy cum pouring out. The seafoam of ten men's cum begins to slide down her thighs as Darrell watches.

He's just about there.

Brokston jogs over from where Zoe's getting eaten and asks Darrell, "Need a hand?"

"Yeah," Darrell answers gratefully, grabbing at his swollen junk and momentarily pleased he's got a hard-on.

Dara turns around just as Brokston and Clark help him to his feet.

"Need to make a deposit, stallion?" Clark winks.

"Spread 'em," Darrell barks at Dara.

Dara gives a knowing smirk with a dark chuckle.

Darrell sort of lurches forward bumping his pelvis with hers.

She slaps her hands against the tile wall. "Fill me up!" she commands Darrell.

My pleasure. Darrell scoops cum from her backside and uses the hot cream liberally on the length of his cock, ramming his hand back and forth, abusing his junk and getting the stiffy he'll need to do the deed.

It doesn't take long with the kind of handwork Darrell applies before his release backs up in his balls like a bomb ready to detonate.

Biting back a hoarse shout, he lines up his prick with Dara's cum-soaked hole and drives his erection deep.

"Ah!" Dara cries, body bucking forward.

He begins to piston insider her wet pussy and only manages about a half-dozen strokes before the bomb of his balls blasts his juice deep.

Wrapping his arms around her, Darrell cups her breasts, still moving deep inside and so zoned he barely hears the locker door open until a feminine voice happily calls out, "I'm here for my exam!"

Dara and Darrell turn to look at the newest person to arrive.

Darrell groans.

Isabella.

Ms. Vanilla of the Year.

GAG REFLEX
A Dara Nichols World Novelette
Volume 6

New York Times BESTSELLER
MARATA EROS

Copyright © 2021 by Marata Eros
All rights reserved.
No part of this book may be reproduced in any form or by any electronic or mechanical means, including information storage and retrieval systems, without written permission from the author, except for the use of brief quotations in a book review.

16

DARA

D ARA GLANCES UP as the door opens and Isabella wanders into the melee.

Her friend halts, mouth forming a small "o" gasp.

Lush blonde hair falls down her back in waves that end in spiral curls along a nipped waist. Her simple outfit: jet-black pencil skirt, heels to match and icy lavender low-cut blouse, suit the situation.

After all, access is key.

Like a lot of people who hail from Scandinavian descent, Isabella is blessed with pool water blue eyes. They widen at the plethora of men in various states of partially disrobed.

Well, isn't this a pickle?

Brokston jogs over to the door, cock bobbing in a most distracting way.

Isabella attempts to keep her eyes on his face, but appears to have them glued much lower.

"Hello, Miss—" Brokston begins while Dara hastily detaches herself from Darrell and attempts to straighten what little bit of the outfit she began with.

"Larsen," Isabella answers slowly, light eyes still pegged at his equipment.

Dara stands. Frowns, *I'm feeling a little bow-legged*, she thinks with a muffled, giddy giggle.

Slipping her high heels back on, she clickity-clacks in Isabella's direction, who is doing the backward lean and bottom lip bite.

Oh dear, her vanilla friend is *really* not into it.

Dara glances down at Brokston's dangling appendage and sighs. It's all well and good for Dara and Zoe but she had hoped to ease Isabella into their fun with a bit more finesse.

Did she give her the wrong time? Dara muses.

Isabella moves her hand as if to take hold of the door handle and bolt. "I, ah—"

Dara inserts herself, giving Brokston a hard shove and he stumbles backward.

Sometimes one must do things themselves.

"Back off stud, let me smooth Isabella's ruffled feathers." She flicks her wild red hair over her shoulder, leveling a calming look at her skittish friend.

"Dara, this is a *lot*—I won't lie."

Dara smirks, *Isabella's not wrong.* "Yes, yes, it is."

Isabella gives a helpless little shrug. "I thought when you said there'd be a little 'hanky-pank' we were talking about a three or foursome."

Hmmm. If pressed Dara always elects a *more-sum.*

Isabella's pale blue eyes roam the general disarray of ten, half-naked doctors plus the trio they began with (good 'ol Clark, Meyers and Brokston—now disgruntled behind her) and of course, Darrell (who had not been expressly invited).

Dara takes a stab at logic, a strong suit of hers. "You

conveyed your apprehension about traveling abroad without the proper inoculations and exams, yes?"

Isabella gives a reluctant nod.

Dara switches to Norwegian, as Isabella is bilingual. "Didn't we have a little 'hanky-pank' with a certain pair of Vikings not too long ago, eh?"

Dara's pussy moistens at the memory of that event.

Color heats Isabella's peaches-and-cream complexion, a charming pink warming her high cheekbones. "Ja," she replies.

"Well, if that's the case," Dara juts out a hip, "just pretend these roosters are the Vikings and only allow a certain number to 'examine' you."

"Wow, that's hot—being all foreign and shit," Darrell says from Dara's elbow.

Dara gives him her profile, switching back to English. "Be a good boy and go check on Zoe."

Isabella peruses Darrell, having to look way up (because, though Dara is tall for a woman at nearly five foot eight, Darrell towers over her at a massive six and a half feet of firefighter love).

Darrell hesitates and with a tapered nail she taps the end of his semi-hard dick. "Shoo."

He glares at her. *Well, my... my.*

"Zoe's fine." His eyes return to Isabella. "I don't think we've been formerly introduced. I'm Darrell," he says, not waiting for Dara to seat the introductions.

Naughty. If Darrell is so anxious...

Isabella licks her lips and Dara's own curve with a calculating thought. *What if?*

"Hey!" Zoe calls out loudly, rudely interrupting Dara's delicate maneuvering.

Dara ignores her.

She is deeply embroiled in sexual negotiation, and with a friend like Isabella, who is so inexperienced, Dara must set the stage for the future.

She cannot have friends dropping like proverbial flies from her shenanigans. That simply will not do.

"Darrell," Dara says, tapping her chin with a blood-red nail tip, "I need *you* to supervise Isabella's team as they examine her."

Isabella blanches.

Dara's finger whips out and presses against her friend's lips. "Silence, sexy—let Dara work her magic."

She lets her finger fall as Darrell runs a tongue over his full, bottom lip. "That sounds reasonable."

Dara smirks. *I'm sure.* Darrell's dark eyes haven't stopped running up and down Isabella since the moment she sauntered in the door.

And, isn't it just a *bit* titillating that our Isabella is a mite reluctant?

Dara thinks so. And really? That's all that matters to Dara.

After all, it's all about her.

"I don't know, Dara," Isabella says, slightly frantic eyes taking in the assembled group, "they all seem a mite *eager*."

Brokston comes to stand behind Dara (apparently past his miff of earlier) and wraps his arms around her torso, pressing her breasts together, mounding them high between his biceps.

His fingers find her pussy lips and spread them.

"Do you want the doctors to be indifferent about your health?"

Isabella is gazing at Brokston's "eager" fingers as they pull her lower lips apart, and he begins exploring how quickly he can work her cum-drenched clit.

Dara lets her head fall back against Brokston's shoulder, relaxing into his maneuvering. "Keep that up, doctor."

"That's the plan, Ms. Nichols," he replies like the compliant male he is. That works because Dara's not keen on another type.

"Let Darrell play neutral and make sure there is quality control of your healthcare."

The other doctors draw nearer and Dara smiles, her breath coming faster as Brokston tramps down hard on her clit.

"Ooh!" she gasps, her pussy beginning to aggressively pulse.

Brokston dips two fingers into her inner cunt as her channel clenches around his impaled digits.

"Oh my God," he says, voice shaky, "she's got a luscious honeypot."

Eyes fluttering, Dara answers, "Yes." Her gaze moves to Isabella. "Surely you can see the high degree of care *I'm* receiving."

"Yes," Isabella whispers, tongue licking her bottom lip. "May I investigate how you've reacted to the treatment?"

Dara nods, a slow smile spreading across her face. Isabella is coming around.

Brokston holds her tightly as Dara spreads her legs.

Isabella strokes a finger down the center of Dara's slick, splayed labia and delicately, with a finesse that makes Dara run even hotter, dips her finger inside her slickness.

"Oh!" Isabella exclaims. "You are—"

Wet, cum-soaked, happy-and-hot, horny as fuck.

All of the above.

"—very well."

Not how Dara would have said things but in a pinch, it'll do.

"My result is typical of the fine care I receive from the doctors of this practice," Dara states in a voice still breathy from climax.

Pupils dilated, Isabella looks at the crowd of swinging, *eager* dicks that pool loosely around her, throat moving up and down in a convulsive gulp.

"Maybe I *could* be examined." She gently gnaws at her lower lip.

Baritone murmuring strikes up.

Dara smiles; she'll be examined all right.

Just then Zoe pushes through the crowd, shooting Darrell a dirty look. "My man is very interested in supervising this slut's exam."

Isabella narrows her eyes at Zoe (who is known for being precocious at the most inopportune of times. Like now.)

In a bored voice, Dara commands to the men at large. "Doctors."

The low chatter stops, pleasing Dara immensely.

"I believe Ms. Scott needs a most thorough exam. Beginning with your primary tools."

Zoe's eyes razor down on Dara. "Wait a fucking second, Dara."

No, Dara needs to quiet Zoe so she might concentrate on Isabell's care.

"Your gag reflex might be in question," Clark says with clear insight, giving Zoe a direct stare.

"What?!" Zoe sputters, hands fisting at her sides.

Darrell chimes in with, "She *could* use more practice."

Zoe's face whips in his direction, aghast.

Excellent.

"And speaking of gags," Dara begins, eyes searching the

doctor's faces for one who might be a thinker instead of just a doer in the group.

The black stallion of the huge junk smiles, holding up the ball that will fit most smoothly in cantankerous Zoe's craw.

Another doctor lifts a hand with a handy pair of handcuffs attached.

Dara adores a prepared male.

"I am Not. Interested." Zoe folds slim arms beneath huge breasts. "Ball gags are a pain in my ass."

Perhaps not quite there, Dara thinks but doesn't say. "Now Zoe," she asserts reasonably, "You know to be invited you must play along."

The women regard each other for a moment and Zoe actually stomps a bare foot, heels long gone at this stage, Dara notices with amusement.

"I think a modicum of silence is warranted here, right boys?"

They all chime acquiesce, Darrell the loudest.

"Fine, you fucking dictator." Zoe pouts.

Dara grins. *Off to the races.*

The men move in, leading Isabella to the community shower for a most thorough exam.

17

ISABELLA

ISABELLA LIKES WOMEN. That's why, when Dara offered up her slick womanhood for examination, Isabella was delighted to check.

Unfortunately, there's just nothing like the hot beef fuel injection. Strap-ons are lovely, but truth be told, they're just not the same.

Isabella allows herself to be tugged to the center of a huge, community shower. The water appears to have been going on and on for some time, as steam billows from the combined streams of at least nine showerheads.

Isabella glances at her lightweight linen ebony pencil skirt and frowns. Likewise with the Italian heels she paid a pretty penny for.

Now, she's not a stupid woman. She *knows* how Dara's tastes run to the ... exotic. However, she was unprepared for this level of fun.

Her pale violet silk blouse begins to cling from the damp environment, her naturally curly blonde hair springing to attention, small tendrils cupping her nape.

The handsome black firefighter moves in behind her and wrapping long fingers around her upper arms he begins to trail soft, hot kisses along her throat.

A gurgled sound reaches her lips and it's with a sort of dull pleasure when she notes Zoe is being thoroughly examined by another black stud who's plunging his mammoth dick into her pussy. Zoe doesn't seem to mind, but the ball gag keeps a lot of her grunts of pleasure and pussy-getting-owned down to a dull roar.

Isabella makes sure the front of her body is in full view of Zoe, whose on her hands and knees and audience to *her* man servicing Isabella.

She deserves the view for fingering Isabella as a slut. *Who is she to talk?*

Darrell moves around to her front and begins unbuttoning her low-cut blouse. When the last button is undone, he brushes the top of the garment from her shoulders and it whispers to the tile.

Without the clothing, her nipples chill in the heated air, becoming erect peaks.

When the other men close in around Isabella in a loose circle formation, Isabella sighs, leaning her head back against whomever holds her.

Warm bodies swirl around Isabella, big hands latching onto her breasts through the lace cups.

Agile fingers unsnap the hook and her breasts fall free into willing hands.

"My God, look at those pretty pink nipples," says one man looming over Darrell's shoulder.

His bright blue eyes scan her round breasts, taking in the peaked nipples.

Pushing Darrell aside he bends his dark head over one and cupping the bottom of her breast he takes the entire nipple into his mouth. A thread of electric lust zings with each pull from his lips, shooting directly to her pussy, causing a throbbing ache to begin in time to his suckling.

"Ooh, that feels *sublime*," Isabella whispers.

Darrell follows Blue Eyes, dipping his equally dark head to give wet, hot attention to the other breast.

Isabella moans from the duality, her pussy aching for something; needing to be filled.

Needing to be *fucked*.

Dara moves in close. "How are you liking the examination so far, Bella?"

"It's magnificent," she replies in a breathy voice.

"Do I have your permission to check if what they're doing is satisfactory?"

Isabella's luminescent blue eyes meet Dara's bright green ones in a moment of perfect understanding. "Oh yes, please do."

"Boys," Dara says and without instruction, hands pinch the skirt's button at her waist, releasing the circular disc from the button hole. The zipper makes a low hiss as it relinquishes her hips to hands against her bare skin.

Her naughty g-string bisects her butt cheeks and a large finger moves it aside.

Maintaining eye contact, Dara slides her finger deep inside Isabella's wet well.

The other woman begins to pump her slim finger inside. "Oh my, you feel very wet, my friend."

"Let me examine her, Ms. Nichols—after all, we don't want to be negligent in our duties." His brown eyes twinkle. "We take our oath very seriously; First, do no harm."

"Well said." Dara reluctantly extracts her finger that's loaded with Isabella's pussy cream.

Brown Eyes takes her finger and engulfs it in his mouth in a slow, erotica pull.

Their eyes lock and he says, "All you women have the sweetest juices."

Dara's eyelashes flutter. "Why thank you, Dr. Meyers." Holding out a hand, an unseen male slaps a towel into her open palm, which Dara precisely folds into a rectangle.

A muffled shout sounds and Isabella's attention is riveted between the two men sucking her tits to a gagged and pleasured Zoe as the huge black man's dick finishes inside her.

Dragging the humongous member from Zoe's drenched snatch, he slaps his softening cock on her lower back, her knees buffeted by a similar towel against the hard tile floor to the one Dara holds.

Isabella's gaze snaps back to Dara, who is laying a towel with precision on the floor right before her.

"Gents, lie down," Dara commands.

Darrell and Blue Eyes lie down on the cold floor.

"Knees on the towel, gorgeous," Dara says lightly, looking directly at her.

Isabella complies, sinking to her knees on the towel and placing her hands on the slightly damp tiles.

Fingers splay at her lower back, hooking a finger beneath the "T" where her G-string bisects her ass. With a hard jerk, the fragile material tears, her butt cheeks jiggling from the movement.

"Ah!" Isabella gasps, training her head to the guy who wrecked her panties.

Just as she turns, a finger plunges into her cunt and she moans at the exquisite sensation, caring less about being de-pantied, and more about the finger pumping inside her wet core.

Isabella begins to push back against the finger.

"She's ready," the man who's pushing his digit deep, says.

Her breasts hang like ripe cantaloupes, gently swaying with her movements and begging to be sucked.

Thankfully, Blue Eyes and Darrell come to her rescue, lying beneath her swinging pendulums, they each grip one of her ripe melons and begin to suck her tits.

"Oh my God," Isabella breathes at the sensation of being sucked and finger-fucked.

"Time for your *first* examination," Dara purrs from her ear and Isabella turns her head to where Dara kneels beside her.

Dara intuits the clear invitation and their lips touch, Dara fisting Isabella's heavy blonde tendrils. Dara Frenchs like no other, twining her silky heated tongue, mining the depths of Isabella's mouth just as the first hot inch of cock begins to breach her entrance.

"She's tight!" the man who's starting to fuck her wet cunt grunts. "I'm trying to fit in."

Dara breaks the kiss, looking deep into Isabella's eyes. "Relax, so the doctors can exam you."

Isabella finally gives in, lying her face against the moist tile, Darrell and Blue Eyes move with her, scooting down to still get at her tits, mounding the globes and taking in even more than her nipple.

Writhing from the attention, the cock in her pussy keeps sinking deeper and deeper.

"Let me at that *slut*," Zoe pipes in.

Isabella's eyes fly open at the sound of the aggressive, pissed-off voice of the woman whose man is lying on the floor, lapping and sucking Isabella's tits.

"Just about there," the guy in her twat announces as his prick kisses the mouth of her womb.

With a wicked smile Zoe cruises behind her—where Isabelle can't see.

"No—hey, I'm sorry about Darrell!" Isabella gasps.

Darrell moans beneath Isabella, never pausing his lush attention.

Great.

Dara sits back on her heels, happily surveying the situation. "Don't worry about Zoe, Isabella—she likes playing nurse." Dara cocks her head, the long fall of auburn hair flowing to her waist. "Don't you, Zoe?"

"Oh yes," she says in a determined voice from behind Isabella.

"Fuck yeah, she's like a vacuum," Brown Eyes says, pulling almost all the way out then impaling Isabella again.

"Gah!" Isabella cries, tossing her head back in pure pleasure at getting owned.

The doctor begins a slow, delicious pounding of her pussy. Isabella is so caught up in his thoroughness, she almost doesn't notice the slick slide of cool gel that lands right above his cock.

Directly above her rosebud.

She lifts her head, the men sucking her tits following her movement.

Craning her neck, the vision of a pissed off Zoe holding a gigantic dildo singes her retinas.

Isabella opens her mouth to say *no way*—she's never had anything up her ass.

A real cock; a fake one. *Never.*

When a doctor kneels in front of her face and says, "It's time for me to test your reflexes,"

Her face swings around and he taps her lips with the tip of his prick.

"What reflex?" she asks in a hesitant voice.

"Gag," Zoe says from behind her as the sensation of something large teases the opening to her ass bud while simultaneously the head of the doctor's cock in front of her begs entry to her closed lips.

Isabella opens her mouth to receive her first exam.

18

ZOE

I'LL SHOW HER, Zoe thinks with great satisfaction. Isabella has always rankled Zoe. Blonde's always been a little *too* above her station.

Won't play games with Dara and Zoe.

Then the ultimate insult comes when Dara invites *Isabella* to travel with only *her*. Doesn't matter that Zoe and Dara have traveled together before. It's just the new exclusivity that hurts Zoe's feelings.

Remembering Dara saying that it was Isabella's turn; that *Isabella* hasn't had a chance at foreign cock.

Isabella this—Isabella *that*.

Of course, Zoe understands her recounting of the conversation might be slightly skewed. Well, this is Zoe's opportunity to loop reluctant Isabella to Zoe's grand scheme of things.

Her way.

Meyers is buried deep in Isabella's hot pink cunt so Zoe aims to make things a bit more *snug*.

Zoe locks eyes with a doctor (whose name she didn't

catch—no worries) who has begun the cock kiss of the moment.

Isabella doesn't appear at first as though she's wanting all the attention, then in a sweep of lucky submission, Isabella opens her mouth to accept the ready cock.

The doctor dude starts a slow fucking of Isabella's mouth, allowing Zoe to concentrate on honing in on her untried ass.

This well-used dildo will to the trick, breaking Isabella in to her first exam properly.

Dara studies the development with avid interest. "Oh my, this will be so dee-lish to watch."

Dara gives a squeal of excitement.

Meyers is pumping away. "I'd love to go bareback," he states in an offhand manner.

"Why not?" Dara quips, "we've all been tested and cream pie is always best served as a hot dish."

Zoe loves Dara methods. She consistently takes the games to a new level, never backs down and always lets stuff happen she shouldn't.

Unpredictability is key for the heat index, in Zoe's opinion.

Isabella tries to comment but it's a difficult option when one's mouth is full of prick.

Unloading a huge amount of lube on Isabella's undulating ass bud, Zoe begins to work just the tip of the huge toy into Isabella's obvious virgin ass.

Her ripe, pink hole starts eating the head of the huge soft cock.

Naturally, Zoe stuffs in more.

"Oh my God—virgin tight, Ms. Scott." Meyers plunges ruthlessly inside as Zoe inserts the dildo midway into Isabella's ass.

She begins loudly moaning around the cock in her mouth.

"I believe Isabella is trying to say something?" Dara comments with a clear lack of real interest, thoughtfully tapping her bright crimson nail tip to her bottom lip.

Meyers withdraws, and in one smooth motion tears off his condom, plunging back inside. "Yeah!" he says gleefully, "that's *so* much better."

Just a bit more, Zoe thinks, sinking the huge dong deeper inside Isabella's ass.

Isabella yells around the dick buried down her throat.

Zoe keeps sinking the huge thing deep, finally burying it to the hilt.

Meyers starts really laying pipe, stiffening as he thrusts a final time.

Zoe keeps hold of the dong, continuing to screw Isabella's ass thoroughly.

The doc at Isabella's face fists her lush blonde hair, driving her lips to his base, unloading his cum deep.

Isabella swallows, gripping his butt cheeks as though to get away from the plunging cocks unloading their wet jizm down her throat and hole. But the dude at the front is not near done unloading and Meyers is slowly pumping to get all that he can inside Isabella's drenched cunt.

Zoe leaves the dong fulling loaded in Isabella's ass, just the jumbo fake nuts spring forth from the ass-end of her engorged hot pink crack.

Meyers finally pulls out with a satisfied grunt and smacks her ass, causing the dong to shiver in place from its impaled position.

"Eat her cunt," Dara directs at Darrell.

Darrell scoots low and catches Zoe's eyes.

Yes, Zoe thinks, *I'll own her ass while my over-eager man eats her pussy.*

"Please," Isabella says, "I don't think I can handle anything more!"

Riiight. Zoe immediately dismisses and begins to pump the huge soaking dong in slow strokes as Darrell puts his excellent pussy gorging skills to the test.

"Ooooh!" Isabella exclaims breathily.

Dara gives Zoe a knowing look as Zoe begins to ream Isabella's virgin ass and Darrell makes the tongue thrust and clit swirl an end-goal.

Isabella begins to subtly push her hips back, her pink assbud sucking in the huge dong.

Dara puts her finger to her lips.

Zoe nods, gloating.

From out of nowhere Dara holds up a strap on, giving a evil little giggle as she twirls it in a semi-circle on her fingers.

Zoe's eyes widen at the length. *Wow.*

"I'm going to do my *own* exam," Dara murmurs and the men crowd her, helping her put on the tight strap on with a nodding, enormous dong at its center.

When finally affixed around her slim hips Dara whips her hips up and down with a short laugh of satisfaction when the dong slaps her upper thigh.

Meyers cum drips from Isabella's slightly used pussy and doctors stand at the ready as Dara begins to insert the ten-incher inside Isabella.

"Oh. My. God," Isabella breathes.

But like the little slut Zoe thinks Isabella is, she doesn't say *no.*

Dara smirks, pumping her hips as she pushes the dong at the end of her tight strap-on into Isabella's cunt.

Zoe keeps up with the dong and with a mighty push, Dara and Zoe thrust, burying the dual fake cocks deep as Isabella shouts, "Coming!" tossing her head back and rocking her spread, whore-cunt back to receive the huge fake toys all the way inside, getting her slutty pussy and ass completely owned and taken.

"What did she say?" Zoe asks, still burying the cock to the core inside Isabella's ass.

"Norwegian," Dara explains in a slightly-out-of-breath voice, swinging her hips forward to meet Isabella's pussy grab.

Huh. Zoe gently withdraws the lubed dong, handing it to a waiting doctor.

Dara finally withdraws from Isabella's ripe pink pussy and another doctor immediately takes her place, his hand already jerking his junk to promote his cream to flow.

With another couple of hard hand pulls he inserts his stiff shaft into her still-pulsing pussy and a handful of thrusts later his body planks as he groans above her.

Isabella spreads her legs further, allowing Darrell better access to her soaking, spread labia.

Zoe knows how fun it is to get licked by Darrell but thinks it's high time she take a turn to show Dara's friend what she's been missing.

"Baby, stop eating Isabella and let someone else have a chance," Zoe pouts.

"I can't take any more," Isabella says, "I mean I came—and I feel like I've been examined, *um*-thoroughly."

"I'm afraid there is not enough proof of exams quite yet," Dara states in a matter-of-fact tone.

Zoe gets a wet(ter) pussy from watching the line-up of male doctors. She notes with a teeny thrill that the big black stallion's at the back of the line.

Zoe understands he wants Isabella's pussy when it's been loosened by the cum train-gang.

Dara walks over to the towel that Zoe had her knees on when the black stallion gave her the biggest cock she'd ever taken. She perches on the towel and sings over to the men who line up behind Isabella, "Come get your back ends checked! Free gag reflex screening," Dara chimes enthusiastically.

Her strap-on glistens from Isabella's twat juice.

Zoe's full lips curve, giving a small head shake of disbelief. Dara is innovative-as-fuck.

Turning her attention to the men lining up behind Isabella, Darrell has conveniently evacuated his position and like a good boy, gone directly to Dara to get his gag reflex checked.

Zoe frowns, he sure seems to be *surrendering* a lot to Dara lately.

With a shrug Zoe scoots underneath Isabella and with a quick idea says, "One on each end."

Cum dumpster time, a Zoe fave.

Zoe wants a reverse, birdseye view and positions herself *just so* beneath Isabella where she can twist those titties, lick that snatch and watch the men unload in her somewhat-reluctant cunt.

"Now wait a moment," Isabella says, as the set of a dozen of so docs split, one group taking the mouth end and the other taking the dual holes at the back.

"Make sure if you fuck her ass bud, that you don't do that first!" Sometimes men have to be reminded of some basic facts.

"I know my sequence!" Brokston chirps as he lines his cock up behind Isabella's hole, plunging deep.

Zoe begins her ministrations, plucking and tweaking first one nipple then the next.

"I-I," Isabella starts but Zoe's already started sucking on her rigid clit, flicking and sucking alternately.

"Oh... Zoe," Isabella murmurs before the first doc sets the tip of his cock to her lips and she opens her mouth to slide his rod of silk to fucking her mouth.

Isabella grunts at the intrusion but as Zoe watches, Brokston has set the precedent for the other men.

After a rough fucking of her cunt, he then moves to her ass, and Isabella's no longer virgin assbud.

Brokston strokes inside, bottoming out in about ten thrusts, where he unloads everything he's got in her pink, dripping ass bud.

When the next doctor moves up behind Brokston for his turn, Isabella sighs, cum leaking down her thighs to overflowing.

The men will all take turns on first, her pussy—then finishing in her ass. Isabella will be so full of cum she won't be able to hold it all.

Just thinking about it makes Zoe's legs flop open as she works the other woman toward a shattering orgasm.

Maybe something will find its way between her legs too.... Zoe smiles around the other woman's clit, enjoying the scorching view.

19

DARA

DARA UNDERSTANDS THAT Darrell needs a bit of discipline for crashing her exam party.

Dara is always at-the-ready for that. After all, she deals with young adult students for her job and has found just the right brand.

Her protocol is very effective.

Hearing muffled grunting, Dara turns where Isabella is now being taken care of by a line-up of fine physicians bent on servicing her with plenty of cream injections.

Who says inoculations have to be bad?

However, a few of the men who she called over before Isabella started getting examined are now in tow.

"Darrell, I'm afraid you can't get away with denying your medical needs."

"But," Darrell gestures to where Isabella's getting *examined* with clear regret etching his features, "I wanted to supervise Isabella's exams..."

Dara doesn't believe that's exactly true. "Now Darrell, I intuit what you actually wanted was to have a turn burying your tool to the hilt inside Isabella and using her as a cum dumpster."

Dara arches a deep auburn brow.

Darrell scowls then finally gives a down and dirty single nod.

"Excellent transparency." Dara turns to the two docs who seemed the most eager to rid themselves of bodily fluids and gives a nod of her own, which is definitely holds a different significance than Darrell's.

"Darrell?"

He places hands on his naked hips, attempting to intimidate Dara with a steadfast glare.

She sees he will need a firm hand.

Or dick, as the case might be.

"Boys," Dara says, crooking a finger.

One of the docs plucks the pair of handcuffs Dara had sighted earlier from the deep white pocket of his doctor's smock, though that is his only attire, Dara happily notes.

Darrell throws up his palms. "Now wait a second."

Dara smiles, tapping her bottom lip with a blood red nail. "Don't be obstinate." Dara allows a small frown to mar the perfection of her forehead. "Was it not you who barged in here and interrupted my exam?" Dara presses her slim fingers between her naked breasts, feels a flake of cum underneath a finger and casually flicks it away.

Darrell's eyes follow the dried cum on its way to the floor.

Dara snaps her fingers and his face jerks up. "Yes or no?"

"I suppose I could have waited for an invitation or reached out before showing up," he mutters almost to himself.

Dara claps her hands together and he startles at the loud smack of flesh on flesh. "Excellent. So you're fully aware that you will need to have a thorough exam. We can't just allow you to be a part of the proceedings and assist the doctor's all the time without yourself submitting to care?"

Her circular argument has teeth and she watches Darrell think through his options, *which are quite limited*, Dara thinks. Being as how this entire exam has been crafted by herself.

Slowly, his eyes fall to the strap on she still wears.

"You're not thinking of being a part of the exam, are you?"

Dara had not mentally gone that far but now that he put the seed of the idea insider her busy brain, she very much likes it.

"Why yes, if the good doctors feel so-moved for assistance from a psuedo-nurse like myself..." Dara chuckles, fully engaged in the *fun* potential, "then I will be fully ready."

"I don't know." Darrell eyes the cuffs in the doctor's hand with obvious uncertainty.

Sometimes another person needs to take away the choices from the subject to push the event along.

With a significant eye flick at Cuff Doc he steps forward and slaps the metal circles on Darrell's wrists.

Dara understands that deep-down, a part of Darrell likes getting owned. And he doesn't seem to need only feminine attention.

That much is apparent as his sizable cock begins its slow ascent to rigid before her eyes.

"Hands and knees," Dara instructs with a congenial smile.

She loves a bit of male flesh at the end of her strap-on once in awhile.

As soon as he drops to the handy towel laid out on the

hard tile that has been conveniently rolled to buffer knee strain, Dara takes position behind Darrell.

Without warning Dara slaps the muscular globe of his ass cheek, his dark meat shivering as he cries out.

Not in pain, she plainly hears—but in excitement.

Gooseflesh erupts from the blow and a dark handprint surfaces.

Dara licks her lips, dramatically holding a tube of lube over the stiff strap-on and inelegantly squeezing a hefty dollop along the length.

There.

Dara places a hand on each butt cheek and begins to spread Darrell's luscious bright pink assbud.

Darrell begins to lower his head.

Dara meets the eyes of Cuff Doctor and with a wink he grabs his junk and flips the tip at Darrell, lightly brandishing his cock against his face.

"Take it, Darrell," Dara sings as she begins the slow tease of the fake shlong that was just parked in Isabella's twat inside Darrell's narrow, tight ass.

"Ahh," he groans, shuddering as Dara deftly begins a slow, inch-by-inch pump of Zoe's black stallion.

Meanwhile, Cuff Doc also begins the simultaneous prick-feed in Darrell's eager mouth.

Because make no mistake, Darrell is making little pleasure grunts as he establishes a rhythm with the other man, cupping his balls and slamming his sensual full lips to the root of the other.

Dara begins to pump his ass in earnest. When things get a little caught, she pours on more lube until his ass is a slick highway of well-tooled flesh.

Darrell begins to push back against the dong and Dar

doubles-down on his ass, ramming the huge fake cock deep in his black hole.

All at once Cuff Dock gives a groan of sheer pleasure and stills while Darrell gobbles all the cum he can shoot into Zoe's man.

Dara gives a last thrust, feeling damn proud about burying the huge cock nearly all the way and leaning over, she cups Darrell's nuts, giving a gentle squeeze.

Giving a hoarse shout he begins to come in great squirts, pouring his cream onto the tile as his body helplessly thrusts at nothing and Dara takes the reins, sliding her hand to his tip and grabbing his cum and working his cock to expel every precious drop.

When Darrell half-collapses on the tile, Dara carefully withdraws the huge tool from his used ass.

"God *damn,* Dara."

Dara looks down at Darrell, allowing a small, Mona Lisa smile to emerge.

"You're so pleased with yourself," he sulks.

"Why yes I am." Dara gives him wide, innocent eyes.

Spinning, she turns away, having done the discipline she set out to do in fine style.

As luck would have it, the last of the males are just finishing up inside Isabella as she makes a study of moaning.

Lovely. Dara saunters over to the group and without so much as a hello, whips to the tail-end of the doctor whose piston pumping is causing Isabella's breasts to plunge back and forward like a locomotive.

Dara quietly lines up behind him and *viola,* she nudges his ass bud with the strap-on.

He stills his forward momentum. "What the....?"

"Surprise!" Dara calls out triumphantly, "I'm an equal-opportunity doer," she says, pushing in with all the finesse of a hippo.

"Hey!" the faceless Doc cries out, ass cheeks clenching.

Dara has the fix, wrapping her long arm around him she brailles out his nutsack and like a repeat of Darrell, squeezes.

"Ah!" he bellows as she sinks another couple of inches of the insatiable dong inside his unwilling hole.

"Da-ra! Da-ra! Da-*ra*!" the other doctors begin to chant. However, Dara doesn't have time for bowing, being a big believer in *follow-through.*

There's so much lube piled on the thing she could screw anything.

Isabella tries to crawl away but she's the anchor holding her subject in place.

We can't have that, she thinks with grim determination.

With a grunt she takes another inch of his ass and he bows forward, parking his dick all the way in Isabella, who mewls from the stiff impaling.

Dara's sweeps her eyes at the loose crowd of Doctors.

She sights down on the one who is nearest and with a jerk of her chin, encourages him to come closer.

When he's within arms reach, Dara grabs him by the smock lapels and pulls him nearer while furiously pumping away.

"Dara!" Isabella says from her hands and knees, "I am tired!' she nearly wails.

Huh. "Not until everyone is empty."

Dara releases the doc and he hurries around to Isabella's front, sinking to his knees he smacks her lips until finally, she relents, allowing the intrusion of his healthy-sized erection to slip inside her hot, wet mouth.

"Even for you, this is a lot," Zoe remarks from her elbow

and Dara grins, running her free hand around the doc's cock and balls as she begins to rhythmically squeeze.

"He'll loosen up about *now*!" Dara announces.

Zoe must sense how close Dara is and without a pause, inserts something hard deep inside her pussy.

The doctor cries out, his ass clamping around the dong and locking Dara in place.

Dara screams, reactively thrusting hard and meeting resistance as the orgasm crashes through her body and the doctor in front of Isabella unloads inside her waiting mouth.

Zoe works whatever she has inside Dara and as her pulses taper off Zoe removes the pleasure tool.

Staggering backward, the strap-on dong slips out of the doctor, who sort of cants to the right and drops to a knee, his spent cock a wet noodle that sticks to the upper side of his thigh.

Breathing hard, Dara backs up against the wall and using it as leverage to hold herself upright, she removes the strap-on one handed and lets it fall to the floor.

Surveying the room, Dara decides that with the examinations coming to an end, she'll be ready for the finale phase of the exams.

20

ZOE

"BABY, DON'T BE like this," Darrell says, chasing after her as they all get showered and dressed.

Baby this, baby *that*.

How about he stick to his guns? Wasn't *he* the one that wanted all the vanilla future?

The first sexcapade of Dara's and he's *all in*.

Literally.

"I'm not being like *anything*. I wanted to be examined and it's a typical Dara-event and you show up thinking you'll be all he-man... which is total garbage because you just really want to *play*."

Darrell stops following her and she turns to face him, folding her arms beneath her boobs. "Admit it. You might think," she taps her temple, "that you're interested in something else but when push comes to shove, you want to get off like the rest of us."

"Children," Dara says, looking daisy-fresh in a new outfit, complete with teal skirt, silk black shell blouse and nude heels to match seamless stockings.

Zoe doesn't know how she does it. She managed to

shower and change but it's blue jeans and a henley T for her.

She glances at her Converse sneakers.

Yup. Put a fork in her—she's done. Been done—done others.

Meyers, Brokston and Clark stroll by, and one of them (Zoe gets them so confused because—yeah, which makes her internally giggle) winks at Darrell, who glowers back.

"Somebody's got their nose out of joint," he comments, leaning down and pecking Dara on her cheek.

"Yes, well if you play there needs to be a good attitude."

"Ah-huh," one of the original trio comments.

Darrell's eyes narrow and he slips out of the massive locker room with a chuckle.

Dara turns slimmed down eyes to Darrell. "You intruded and shouldn't be behaving badly. As I recall, you did me and Isabella, it's not like you got the short end of the stick."

Exactly, Zoe thinks. "I wasn't planning on doing anyone."

"You never are," Darrell points out.

"So, you came here to what? Check up on me and all that did was get me back to Neapolitan and you double-dipping."

"I do adore the ice cream analogies," Dara off-handedly comments, still seeing the dozen plus doctors out.

When the dude with the handcuffs walks out last Darrell actually huffs out an exhale.

The doctor turns and gives a mock-salute with his index finger at Darrell.

The big black guy trucks over and chucks Zoe under her chin. "Don't be too hard on him." His grin is very white inside the locker room. "I had you both and there are no favorites," he says.

With that, he walks out and it's just the three of them.

Her eyes find Isabella, applying the last bit of lipstick as she purses lips to the reflection, seemingly not listening to every word they're saying.

Yeah right.

"Maybe you take this vacation with Dara." His dark eyes are steady on Zoe's face.

What? "Dara hasn't invited me, Darrell," Zoe says, carefully not looking Dara's way.

God knows Zoe doesn't want to be a mercy invite.

Isabella walks over and Miss Perfection doesn't look so perfect. Silk gets ruined when wet and her icy purple blouse is spotted and wrinkled, the pencil skirt appears somewhat munched and there's a run in her stockinged left leg.

"Bella and I would be more than happy for Zoe to go with, if her work allows it. I didn't invite her initially because I know summer travel is great for me because I'm not teaching—but not so good for her."

She turns to Dara. "You wanted me to go."

Without a moment's hesitation, Dara steps into her personal space and sinks her hand into Zoe's long, curly hair.

Leaning over her shorter frame, Dara presses soft lips to hers.

They kiss, softness becomes heat as she molds her supple lips to Zoe's, moving over them with deft precision.

Tongues twine then release.

Dara lifts her head. "Never doubt it." She then looks at Darrell. "At the very best, you're conflicted and that just gets on my nerves. If a dozen doctors can play and shake it off but you're here, all full of angst, that doesn't cut it."

Darrell blinks.

Isabella pipes in, "If anyone should object it would be

me." She splays perfectly manicured nails between the collar lapels of her damp blouse. Isabella spreads her arms away from her sides. "I was expecting something different."

Zoe feels a crooked smile seat itself on her lips. "Something less."

She turns to Zoe. "Exactly."

"But Dara," Zoe says.

Darrell grunts. "Yeah, Dara."

Dara watches the exchange with interest. "You came." Dara's grin is sudden. "And boy—did you."

"You knew what it would be Darrell." Zoe stares at him, willing him to be reasonable. Tired of this argument.

"You can't have it both ways, my friend," Isabella comments. "If you want to play, then play. If you want your girlfriend to play, then don't spoil the fun."

"Fun?" Darrell runs a hand over his skull trim and stares at her. "It's fun, but like we'd decided, I want more."

Zoe shakes her head, palm sailing out to encompass the now-quiet showers. "I don't want this all the time."

Dara states softly, "But you want it sometimes."

She gets Zoe. *I love Darrell, I do.* But when he wants to do this shit, interfere, cop an attitude like he wants to be straight and narrow then fuck everyone anyway. *Feel guilty later?*

It's drama lama shit.

"Yeah, I want it when I want it. And you know how Dara rolls, she's already scheming about the next time, right?" Zoe cranks her head to the right, where Dara nonchalantly stands between her and Darrell.

"Yes, as a matter of fact, I've enlisted the help of a new group of doctors for a final exam before Europe."

"Figures," Darrell mutters.

"If you want to join us on one of the legs of our

European trip, feel free. However," Dara's green eyes level on Darrell's expressive face. Right now, his expression is peeved, "if you want to arrive and not go with the flow..."

"Your way?"

Dara graces the three of them with a benign smile. "Is there another?"

"There has been." Darrell frowns. "I remember a certain firehouse...."

"Yes, that was delightful," Dara says instantly.

"But?" Darrell asks, pegging his large hands on his hips.

That's a fighting stance if ever she saw one.

But Dara can handle him. *I think.*

"I'm not after redundant encounters."

"Dara enjoys spontaneity."

"No shit?" Darrell snorts.

"Yes—no shit," Dara says, the swear word sounding oddly out-of-character from her lips.

"Well, I'm out of here," Darrell says, beginning to walk to the door.

"I've extended the invite," she says and he turns, in profile.

"Nice to be included but it'll have to be Zo who wants me. And we've got to hammer out rules."

"Why?" Isabella asks softly. "Why must there be rules?"

"Because that's the way it's gotta be for me," he thumbs the center of his chest and Zoe sighs, watching him go.

Again.

"He is an exciting mix of volatility and submission," Dara remarks, coming to stand next to Zoe, she curls and arm around her shoulders.

"However, at the end of the day, there's just too much work there," Isabella says in an almost mournful tone.

"Agreed," Dara says then turns slightly, taking in what I'm sure is Zoe's woeful expression.

"We have time."

They turn to Isabella. "It will be a hard recovery and then..."

"Then we will explore the last examination protocol."

The corners of her lips quirk. "Uh-huh. I bet."

Dara's smile returns, "He's just a man, Zoe—don't worry about him."

But he was my man, Zoe thinks.

Is she happy he's made a semi-ultimatum, or is she relieved.

Maybe a little of both.

Before Zoe can ponder things too long, Dara loops her arm through Zoe's and Isabella mirrors her on the opposite side.

"Come on now, my friend, let's make plans that don't include boyfriends," Isabella says.

"She's right, you know."

Zoe allows herself to be led from the locker room where so much fun was had.

And lines in the sand were drawn.

HARD RECOVERY
A Dara Nichols World Novelette
Volume 7

New York Times BESTSELLER
MARATA EROS

Copyright © 2022 by Marata Eros
All rights reserved.
No part of this book may be reproduced in any form or by any electronic or mechanical means, including information storage and retrieval systems, without written permission from the author, except for the use of brief quotations in a book review.

21

ZOE

ZOE FOLDS HER arms beneath her breasts. "I thought there would be a *final* exam." She attempts to rein in the pout, badly.

Dara shoots a long-suffering glance in Zoe's direction then shifts her weight on the cupped, hard-as-a-fucking-rock row of seats connected by uninspired once-shiny metal bars.

Noise floods the space, a mix of badly accented English announcers for flights, bratty children and rude people who don't want to be waiting in an airport any more than her.

Dropping a slender wrist on her short, dark cobalt skirt, Dara repositions her forearm from another glance at her shiny watch. "You're just out-of-sorts because you broke up with Darrell," Dara announces as fact.

Zoe purses her lips at her friend's insights. "*He* broke up with me," she admits in a surly tone.

"Not that the dumpee or the dumper must be established," Isabella says from between them, slowly lowering her cell phone, and swiping the book she'd been reading to darkness with a practiced thumb.

"Sounds like someone taking a shit, instead of relationship dismantling," Zoe grumbles.

"Not as I would have put it but I suppose it could be perceived that way."

Isabella snickers.

Zoe glowers at Dara, semi-heaving herself against the stiff chair back. "Why couldn't the big D come at a time when I'm ready to wind my shit down?"

Dara lifts and elegant, silk-encased shoulder in the exact deep blue hue as the skirt. "I don't know that it's reasonable to assume you will ever want to 'wind shit down.'"

"My friend, I do not think the profane suits you," Isabella comments, stretching her legs out before her. Isabella is wearing slacks. Cream-colored merino wool. Or winter white. That's what Dara would call them, Zoe's sure.

For Zoe's part she wears a jumpsuit. And old-fashioned, shoulder pad heavy all-hot pink and perfectly fitted blend of cotton and stretchy spandex.

A thin gold chain with a small puffed heart nestles between her breasts, just so.

Dara's smile upon seeing the sizzling pink ensemble had been worth it. And her comment of "ready for anything" accessorizing.

Zoe had noted the outfit had been just that—*not* an accessory.

Dara's lips had curved as she'd remarked it can become an accessory in the right hands.

Zoe leans forward, letting her hands dangle between her thighs and taps her matching hot pink stiletto to the rhythm of her irritation.

"Okay," she makes a slashing gesture with her palm. "Enough of Darrell."

"He *was* yummy," Isabella murmurs in a dreamy voice.

Zoe gives her a withering look.

"Well," she says, laying her open palm between her boobs, "refute it."

Of course, Zoe can't.

"Nevertheless, our black stallion has moved on to more vanilla pastures," Dara says, picking an invisible piece of lint from her brilliant blue ensemble. "Besides," Dara says with a dismissive wave of her hand, "I've a great bit of news."

Isabella and Zoe exchange a glance. Dara does love dropping news bombs.

"First, there *will* be an exam upon arrival."

Goodie gumdrop, Zoe thinks, charitable thoughts returning.

"And, fortuitously, a favorite Danish great uncle has passed, and that country has very beneficial inheritance laws."

"Like Norway?" Isabella asks lightly, brows popped.

Dara's eyes sparkle. "Exactly like."

"So what does this mean—you've inherited the goat farm?" Zoe barks out a laugh and leaning back again, crosses her screaming pink pantlegs.

Zoe's red-headed friend lets the suspense draw out, pausing only to let the blaring speaker of another flight's last call blare between them.

"Try five million dollars, USD."

"No," Zoe breathes, letting casual pretense fall away to eager interest. Though Zoe makes decent money through her graphic design free-lance gig, it's always a financial stretch to do these "Dara trips" as Zoe has mentally coined them.

"Well it makes room service more affordable," Isabella murmurs.

"Please," Dara says, leaning back and stretching her slim

arm across the unforgiving back of the adjunct seat, "You're old money."

"Too true."

Really? Zoe thinks. *Is she the only working stiff of the three?*

"Zoe, don't look so glum." The corners of Dara's lips tweak. "I share."

Yes she does. But... "What does this mean? Will you keep on being Ms. English?"

Dara's expression morphs to thoughtful. "I do like the eager young bucks who make not the slightest pretense of understanding our complicated native tongue."

"Because you can give them lessons more to your liking," Isabella quips.

Dara inclines her head, a semi-dazed smile affixed to her refined features. "True. Though I've grown bored with the most recent batches of young studs."

What? "What?" Zoe asks, leaning forward. This is the first she's heard of it.

"Craig Taylor has become tiresome, always wanting his slice of 'Dara pie' as he calls it." She makes an inch of space between her index finger and thumb.

"He wasn't *that* small," Zoe says, though he did need excessive discipline, as she remembers it.

"That's not how I heard it," Isabella says with a soft laugh.

I guess he hadn't been that remarkable, now that Zoe thinks back. "I liked giving him his just deserts." She snorts.

Dara gives a sage nod. "Certainly he was a good deal of fun to manipulate..."

"However, he began turning the tables on our Dara," Isabella chimes.

Zoe frowns. "Our Dara," her ass. "How?"

"This last university season he'd drop by at the most

inopportune times. Uncanny timing, and then—of course, I was honor-bound to include him in the fun."

"Which made it way-*less* fun," Zoe guesses.

"Exactly." Dara looks directly at Zoe, "this windfall could not have come at a better time. I tenured my resignation, effective for the new year."

Zoe feels her eyes widen. "Oh shit."

Isabella grins. "No more Dara pie for President Taylor."

"So, let me get this straight. You're tenured, right?"

"Yes, Zoe."

"Okay, I know what you just stated—what do you get out of this, if anything?"

"I have been a university professor for two decades. I am of a certain age." Dara gives another elegant shrug. "I have enough 'time in' to have a sizable enough pension. I could move on—teach elsewhere."

"Europe?" Isabella cocks a platinum brow.

A slow smile begins to spread on Dara's full lips. "Anywhere I wish. I did not burn the Craig Taylor bridge."

Zoe looks at her. "You wanted to?"

"Oh yes—I certainly did." She smooths her hands down her skirt.

"*I* have to keep working," Zoe restates for prosperity.

Isabella and Dara look at her.

Gawd. "Well, I do!"

"But you have how many weeks set aside?" Dara asks.

"Three," Zoe replies slowly, then narrows her eyes on her friend. "What?"

"I've arranged for a few extras now that there's been a loosening of the belt."

Ah-huh. "What extras?"

"You sound *so* suspicious," Isabella remarks, blue eyes wide.

"I know Dara better than you," Zoe states in a dry voice. *Take that.*

Isabella huffs, crossing her arms and attempting to look fierce.

"Well—since we are just past the holiday season and the weather is less-than-desirable, I determined to postpone Europe in favor of a warmer locale."

"And first class," Isabella pipes in.

"I *knew* we were traveling first class," Zoe says, barely restraining the eye roll. "And now you don't have to return after the holiday."

Dara shakes her head, her stick-straight dark auburn hair shimmering with the movement.

"Okay, so under the original plan we were flying into Amsterdam and now we're flying into...?"

"I thought I'd try for frugality."

Zoe does roll her eyes at this stage. "You're never cheap, Dara—you couldn't be cheap if it were a goal."

A light blush rises on her high cheekbones. "I was this time—really, we're flying to Mazatln, Mexico. Bora Bora was out—even with my newfound wealth."

"Que bueno," Isabella remarks.

Zoe's got that. "Yo tambien."

Dara gifts Zoe with a one-hundred watt smile. "I know you understand some Spanish, Zo?"

Zoe winks. "I can get by—but you? Miss Linguist."

"Our Dara will do more than get us by."

Zoe narrows her eyes at Isabella.

"Far more," Dara confirms. "And yes, Spanish is in the romance language grouping."

Translation: Dara can speak Spanish too. No shock there.

Zoe smirks. "I don't think *romance* is in the cards."

"Not the brand of romance that is traditionally thought of, no." Dara leans back, crossing her slender ankles. "We have the standard limo from the airport, the standard massage—and the *not*-so-standard first exam."

"So, we *are* getting a medical exam," Zoe asks, getting a flutter of excitement in her belly.

Zoe loves getting a clean bill of health.

Dara tilts her head just as the tinny voice comes on for a flight that Zoe doesn't recognize but Isabella stands as if on cue.

"You can't expect to travel foreign in the middle of a pandemic and not have some kind of assurance that you're well," Dara states, deadpan.

"Oh my God, Dara—what have you got planned?"

She twirls a mask on her index finger that's fabric is littered with cucumbers and olives.

"Nothing irregular—just complete and utter spoilage. I took time to acquire bikinis for all of us and arranged for a Tres Islas tour."

"Three islands?" Isabella laughs.

Dara's eyes darken in that sly smutty way Zoe loves so much. "They're not inhabited. The only way to see them is to charter a boat." Her wicked smile remains affixed. "I've also arranged catering."

"Food?"

Isabella frowns at Zoe's one word question.

"Some food... and some other things."

Zoe stands, she's ready. Let the shenanigans begin.

Dara scoops her nude clutch from the seat and begins to walk toward the tarmac.

"Wait," Zoe says, trotting after her.

Dara turns just as she slides the passport inside the reader and murmurs politeness.

A affirmative chime sounds and Zoe does the same.

Dara strides down the long corridor leading to the large waiting jet.

"Is there anything I should know about this trip since you switched countries on me?"

Dara gives Zoe her profile and she quickly looks around to see Isabella rushing there way from a few yards behind their position.

"Only that the bikini is the only accessory you'll need on this trip."

Typical Dara. Zoe swallows hard. "What about Europe?"

Dara swirls her hand around dismissively, ducking as she hops inside the plane and absently looks for her seat.

Lifting the upper storage bin open, she rams her clutch inside and slaps it closed with a decisive whack then smoothly maneuvers to a large window seat midway down the isle.

Dara seats herself and Zoe sits beside her.

Isabella manages to finally join them.

Zoe's opens her mouth to pump Dara for more info but a flight attendant is already asking what they'd like to drink.

"Champagne for all three," Dara says, swinging a sleek ebony manicured nail to loop both her and Isabella.

The flight attendant leans down and using a conspirator's whisper, asks, "Are you *the* Dara Nichols."

What?

"The one and only," Dara confirms without missing a beat.

Straightening, the flight attendant gives Dara a special smile. "The captain and first would love to ah..." her eyes dart around the first class cabin as though they're being spied on, "make your acquaintance."

"It sounds as though I already have," Dara says.

The flight attendant blushes, a brushfire of color causing her cheeks to warm and her velvet brown eyes to sparkle.

"When? Because I'm *thirsty*," Dara emphasizes, dropping her normal subtlety for the direct approach.

The blush reignites.

Isabella and Zoe exchange a glance.

"Typically, a mile high," the flight attendant says.

Dara and she lock eyes. "I like the sound of that."

Clearly relieved she says, "Perfect—I'll mention it to the pilots." The flight attendant leaves with a practiced slink of hips.

Relaxing back into her seat, Dara gives a secret smile.

That's when Zoe understands their adventures have already started—before they even land.

22

DARA

"LARGE, PORTABLE HANDHELD and other devices may be turned on at this time. We've now reached our cruising altitude of thirty-five thousand feet."

"A mile high," Zoe chirps at her elbow.

Dara lifts her champagne flute; her and Zoe clink crystal.

"I've done a lot of traveling and this part never gets old," Bella mentions, clinking crystal with them.

Too true.

"Who are the pilots?" Zoe asks.

Dara smirks. "Old friends—you'll see," she says, cagey.

"I peeked inside the cockpit," Bella admits.

Dara grins. Her Bella is insatiably curious. "And?"

"Countrymen."

Zoe's large, dark eyes widen, so fetching when surrounded by all that simmering pink and Dara watches the wheels turn behind those bright eyes as she connects dots. "The vikings?" she fairly squeals, "On our way to Mazatln?"

"Now Zoe—don't wreck my surprises," Dara murmurs.

"Never," she says—properly chastised. And sitting back against the plush seat she mimes zipping her lips and tossing an invisible key.

The flight attendant comes rushing forward, a frosty champagne bottle in hand.

Their fourth, Dara estimates through mental tally. And she is keeping one. Just because she's a professor of English literature does not mean she's unable to count.

Like now; they're a mile high. Timing is everything, she understands.

With a furtive glance around her once more the flight attendant says softly, "The pilots are ah—*available.*"

Zoe raises her empty flute.

Bella (not to be outdrank, it appears) gives just a tiny sway of her hand upon doing the same.

Dara is steady-as-a-rock.

The bubbly shimmers its way into the chilled flutes and the ladies stand.

"Follow me," the flight attendant says with a wink.

"Hey," a masculine voice breaks into Dara's perfect buzz of champagne and light *hors d'oeuvres* that slosh around inside her.

Dara loathes the uncouth.

Turning on her four-inch spike heel a handsome if boorish youngster is half-rising.

The flight attendant halts mid-stride.

"Where are these gals going?" he asks, swinging a finger at Dara and friends.

Bella pops a hip. "Why does that matter to you?"

Before Zoe can join in, as that heralds events trending to pear-shaped, Dara interjects, "We've been invited into the cockpit."

His face says it all. Mollified, resentful and full of self-importance. Dara understands very well how to deal with this sort of male.

With a firm hand.

He straightens to standing and two-strides himself into position next to Dara.

Perfect.

Maneuvering her body to just behind all other passengers' line-of-sight she smoothly cups his balls right through his slacks.

"Hey!" he squeals as he rises on his toes.

Dara increases the pressure slightly, capturing his mossy green eyes with her bright emerald ones. "Don't think you can flounce after us and be part of the fun without an express invitation."

"Let go of me," he says in a squeak.

Dara flutters her eyelashes. "No."

"She hasn't even begun to get after you, sweet thing," Zoe enumerates in her way.

Boorish's eyes tighten. "This isn't fun."

"You should have thought through this eventuality before making a spectacle." Bella's blue eyes flash fire at him.

Coltish as usual, Dara notes.

Dara has stood off with far more intimidating males then this ones nuts she holds within her grasp. As Dara sees it, there's a few nordic studs waiting to become reacquainted with Dara and her pals. If Boorish doesn't want to play *her* way—he doesn't get to play.

"*What*—can you take your hand off my nuts?" he asks in a fierce whisper.

"I *could*. I have the ability, but sadly—no motivation."

Dara starts to work her way up his cock, which unsurprisingly, is rising to the occasion.

"This is the weirdest fucking thing I've ever been a part of," he admits.

"You're not a part of anything, yet," Dara smoothly states.

Their eyes meet again, his breaths coming faster. Dara figures she can bring him in three minutes flat in the middle of the airplane aisle way—or he can see reason and trot after the ladies so there can be a little *flying fun* in the next five minutes.

It's been her experience that men can become a touch antsy if the proverbial ball doesn't begin to roll.

Eyes beginning to glaze he says, "I think I want to be a part..."

"Think or will."

He blinks those lazy forest greens. "Will."

Instantly, Dara releases his junk and he takes a staggering backward step, his slacks comically tented above a healthy erection.

Zoe steps up to the plate and snaps her fingers in his face. "Hello, stud—time to trot."

Dara hides her smile with a fist. Turning on her heel, she makes her way behind the flight attendant (who seeing how Dara maneuvered the young disciple, appears to possess renewed confidence).

Dara doesn't wait to see what he'll end up doing. Shutting him up and sizing him up were the priorities of the moment.

The flight attendant taps a knuckle softly at the cockpit door and a voice says *come.*

In Norwegian.

Dara is all about revisiting fun.

The door opens and Dara squeezes past the flight attendant.

Then in troops Zoe, Bella with Boorish bringing up the rear.

Literally, Dara hopes with a badly contained snicker.

*

"Who's this?" Lars asks, eyeing up Boorish boy (who Dara acknowledges isn't anywhere near underage but young enough to mold, by God).

She casually turns, noting the tightness of the space and wonders if that will be a problem, or aid in the entry.

Aid.

"What's he saying?" Boorish asks.

"I suppose we'll name you," Dara says with a bit of regret. Sometimes nameless men are the only ones she likes.

"I'm Brad."

Bella takes the conversational reins, having an idea of Dara's disinterest in that area. "This is Zoe and I'm Isabella."

His dark green eyes move to the pilots (who Dara thinks of as the Nordic twins).

He grunts. "I don't do dudes."

Dara hikes a thumb in the direction of the cockpit door. "We do, so you will. Or you can go away." Dara makes a shooing gesture with her fingers.

His pupils dilate. "I want to do *you*."

Zoe rolls her expressive brown eyes. "Not very unique, pal; everyone wants Dara."

"Thank you, Zoe," Dara says without turning.

"Pfft, you don't have a big ego or anything," Brad says.

Dara doesn't hide her irritation. "No, I don't. I don't have room for ego, but I have room for all kinds of cocks and tongues. Play or go away."

Brad blinks at her bald speak. "Well—I..."

Dara cocks her head to the right, inspecting the tall and handsome Brad. "Not speaking might be a better option for you."

His lips clamp shut.

In Norwegian Dara rapidly explains that Brad barged in, uninvited and needs his virgin hole waxed for his oafish transgressions.

Hans and Lars both grin. "Ja," Hans says with slow conviction, his vibrant close-cropped red hair vying with Dara's.

Lars claims only Norwegian ancestry and is as blond as Bella.

This will be fun, Dara decides.

"I didn't know the Vikings were pilots," Zoe chimes.

"I don't believe occupations were discussed," Dara concedes. Her eyes run down Brad.

She wants him naked and swinging.

Dara admits she's somewhat incensed to include a stranger when she was thinking she and the girls would be joining the mile high club on their own.

Dara eyes the zipper on Zoe's jumpsuit that begins at the exact depth of her sumptuous cleavage.

"Zoe darling, rid yourself of the top half of your outfit. I've been dying to get a peek."

Zoe's full lips curve, a willing partner in whatever Dara has up her sleeve.

Which is a lot, as things turn out.

Lars smirks. "Dara, look at the newest item we've outfitted the cockpit with."

"I love the name," Zoe says randomly.

Dara's keen on anything with the word "cock" in it.

Hans and Lars part, revealing a lever between their seats.

Perhaps without the extra, the lever would be a solid metal piece with an enamel ball or oblong handle at its peak.

But now, it's been outfitted with a tremendous-girth long dong, clearly hollowed-out to be seated on a permanent *something*.

Standing at staggeringly rigid attention, the toy looms large between the two men.

"Oh," Bella says with a soft gasp of surprise. "That's...."

"Deliciously *huge*," Zoe says with rapt admiration.

Brad guffaws and decision made, Dara turns to him and says, "Before our fun is through, you'll be wearing that as an ass ornament."

He jerks his jaw back. "No way."

"Way," Hans says in Norwegian, giving a protracted wink at his co-pilot, Lars and looping Dara in the expression.

"Who's going first?" Dara asks, eyes sweeping the tight space until she lands on the flight attendant.

Hmmm.

"Are you staying of going?"

"I'm not—I've never..." Her large brown eyes continue to return to the dong.

"Perfect," Zoe says, latching onto the young woman's wrist like a snake with a score to settle.

Lars and Hans grin, moving to surround....

Dara's eyes drop to the slim rectangle nameplate neatly pinned to her uniform's tight vest above her right breast.

Becky.

Dara takes in the young woman. She had not given her much attention before now as she'd struck Dara as an unwilling wilting flower.

"How old are you?"

"Twenty-one. That's the only way I could have served the champagne." She gives a small shrug.

Sometimes Dara gets off watching a new player get broken in.

Like now.

"Becky, we've decided to take you into the fold."

"We have?" Zoe asks, fingers still clamped around Becky's narrow wrist.

Dara shoots Zoe the look that delayed comment deserves.

"We have," she enthuses.

Dara's gaze shifts back to the dark eyes of the young Becky.

"Zoe will show you the ropes and you do as your told."

"I don't know—I mean—what do I have to do?"

With an internal sigh, Dara thinks, *Blindfold*. Because she's a prepared sort, Dara reaches up underneath her skirt and carefully retrieves a folded, satin blindfold—really more mask than blindfold and silently hands it to Becky.

"Put this on and stand still."

"Ah," she bites her lower lip and looks at the pilots. "What about the," she shoots her thumb in the general direction of the plane where she served them drinks earlier.

"We'll take care of that."

Bella steps behind Brad and locks the cockpit door.

Slowly, Becky puts on the blindfold.

Releasing her hold on Becky, Zoe begins to unzip the top part of her jumpsuit and carefully extracts her arms from the sleeves.

Her titties drop out from the tight hold of the bodice and just a heart necklace dangles between them.

Dara is a big fan of Zoe's tits and saunters over to cup

one full boob she dips her head, taking the nipple and beginning to suck on the puckered flesh for all she's worth.

"God, that's hot," says Brad.

Dara had forgotten all about him.

Her mask will do for him, she ruminates. "Brad," Dara says, reluctantly lifting her mouth from Zoe's hot nipple.

"Don't stop, Dara," Zoe says.

Dara hands her mask with cocks masquerading as cucumbers to Brad. "Blindfold time."

"Man, I wanna watch."

Ah-huh. And that is exactly why Brad must be blindfolded.

He stuffs the mask on over his eyes, which suits Dara fine. She returns her wet attention to Zoe.

Dara moves her eyes to Lars and Hans.

They move to Becky and Brad.

"Put your hands up on the wall," Hans instructs Brad in accented English.

"Wait a second, I wanted to be with a girl," he wheedles.

Dara knew her involvement would be necessary.

With an indelicate pop off from Zoe's delectable teat, Dara pivots smoothly and moves up behind Brad.

In a flash, she rams his hands up on the wall, and tucks the front of her pelvis against the back of his ass cheeks.

He groans, his cock mashing into the wall.

"Be a good boy and you'll get off," she says, giving Lars side-eye.

Lars proves his understanding of her unspoken cues by moving forward and grabbing the enormous erection Brad just sprouted.

Hans moves behind Becky and unbuttons her tight, flight attendant skirt, smoothing it past bare hips to pool at her feet.

No panties, Dara thinks about two seconds before the girl covers her pussy with her palms.

Oh for pity's sake. Who goes without panties then tries to cover?

No one, Dara thinks.

Lars spins Brad.

Brad tries to lower his arms.

"Absolutely not, lover boy," Dara says and grabs his nuts for the second through his pants.

Brad grunts.

Lifting her hand so Lars can expertly take down Brad's pants, he reveals boxer briefs sporting a hot cock straining against material with scattered pineapples.

Hans kicks Becky's legs apart and she gasps, nearly losing her footing and pinwheeling her arms to find purchase.

She grasps onto the huge fake dong covering the pilot's lever between the seats.

Attempting to spring up, she misses and falls forward again.

Right on top of the newly seated and depants-ed Hans.

Perfect.

Becky's palms land on his bare thighs with a loud slap and without pause, Hans guides her face to his prick.

"Ohhhh," she says as he lands her lips on the mushroom-tip of him and begins forcing her down his length.

Spread wide and naked for ownership, Lars tears down Brad's pineapple boxers and lines up his cock with a spread Becky.

Her head is bobbing on Hans' dick and without further ado, Brad lines up with Becky's hole and dives right in.

"Argh!" she screams around Hans' cock.

Brad doesn't disappoint, getting the girl he wanted so bad.

Zoe steps forward with handy lube in hand, squirting an obscene amount on Brad's dick, making the spearing of the unsuspecting Becky stab more smoothly.

Now—for the fun part.

Brad is grunting away, doing a perfect piston performance when Dara opens her palm, making a "come here" gesture to Zoe.

Zoe slaps the tube of lube into Dara's hand and with the precision of a surgeon, Dara moves to the huge dong standing at attention at the center of the cockpit and upends half the bottle on the dong.

Her eyes meet those of Lars.

As a team, they'll get Brad exactly where they want him.

Lars, Bella, Zoe and Dara eye up the glistening ten-inch fake dong waiting to impale someone.

As if on cue, Brad stiffens behind a struggling and grunting Becky, who is getting her fair share of cream from both ends.

With a heaving sigh, Brad staggers back, having had his fun—right into the waiting arms of Lars.

"God, that was fucking great—*awesome* pussy," Brad swaggers out.

Dara's lips curve.

Lars pats Brad's head, throwing a muscular arm around his shoulders.

The girls move back to allow him to draw nearer to the dong, then swarm him like busy bees as Lars gently guides him backwards, unwittingly lining Brad virgin rosebud with the ass-fucking of his young life.

23

ISABELLA

Isabella is aroused.

She wasn't sure about Dara's events before the locker room fun, but seeing the young Brad about to get owned by the ginormous fake cock has put her sexual mental engagement right back to center.

Like Brad's ass, she mentally giggles.

"Wait a sec, dude," Brad tries to struggle away but Hans is occupied getting his pole lubed by Becky and Lars is determined to *seat* Brad.

"No, it's time for your happy ending, Brad!" Dara chirps.

Dara's such a character, Isabella thinks; not for the first time.

Lining Brad up isn't too difficult as the cockpit is deplorably small. His flaccid cock slaps against his upper thigh as Lars mutters in her native Norwegian, "There we go! Just... about, *there!*" and with a small triumphant grunt, the juicy top of the dong begins to pierce Brad's virgin ass.

"Hey!" he wails.

Really? Isabella muses, remembering all the fun that was

had in the locker room. Perhaps Brad just doesn't have that adventuress spirit.

"Now *Brad*," Dara begins, sidling between his spread, quivering thighs, "this isn't the time for immaturity. You had your fun with Becky and now we need you to warm up this lovely implement."

"It's gonna hurt my ass!"

"Not if you relax," Dara says in an expert tone, and doing Dara, she tears open her bright blue blouse, buttons smacking the windows of the interior cockpit windows like rice flung at a wedding.

My, my.

Scooping a plump, pale breast from a demi-cup, sheer cobalt bra, Dara shoves her fingers through Brad's short dark hair and pulls his face to her nipple.

Isabella notes his ass succumbs to gravity by at least another inch.

"What?" then Brad's thoughts are pleasantly muffled (he had been a mite chatty for Isabella's taste) and Lars stands at-the-ready to shove his tight assbud down further on the fuckable dong.

"Argh!" Brad groans around Dara's breast as she grabs his soft junk and begins to work it like she means it.

Excellent.

Lars moves behind Brad and places his hands on the young buck's broad shoulders, pushing gently down as he does.

More of the huge dong impales Brad and Isabella estimates about half has been fed into his assbud.

Not wanting to be out in the cold, Isabella cocks a brow at Zoe who's already moving toward Lars.

Isabella sights in on Hans as he finishes inside Becky's hot, wet mouth.

Her eyes run to the backend of Becky where a wee bit of cum has dribbled out of a very pink and tight-looking hole.

Isabella shifts her attention from Becky's tempting pussy and the action before her with a reluctant Brad.

Eeny-meeny-miny-moe.

Isabella is enchanted by the fresh slit presented as Hans groans and offloads inside Becky.

With a determined couple of paces Isabella runs a palm down Becky's bare ass then with a practiced twist and dive, she plunges her finger deep into the other woman's wet well.

"Oh god," Becky says, pulling her plump and swollen lips off Hans' spent cock and meeting Isabella's eyes over her shoulder.

"Bend over, Becky," Isabella says, taking charge *a la* Dara.

Bending over, her pink pussy lips part, giving Isabella all the access she requires. By all appearances, Becky has definitely enjoyed the dual male attention and is compliant.

Slowly sinking to her haunches, Isabella thumbs Becky's pussy apart wide, admiring the glistening juices of her arousal and Brad's recent deposit.

Giving a long lick, the younger woman shivers above Isabella's wet attention and Hans slides out from below her mouth.

Isabella watches as Hans cock begins to grow again as he makes the short distance to just behind Becky.

"I want to fuck her ass," he says in abrupt Norwegian, already working his soft meat to harder before her eyes.

If she can maneuver herself out of the way while still licking and having fun with Becky's used pussy, that completely works for Isabella.

"Viagra is the wonder pill of the ages," Hans adds, his now-impressive erection at full tilt.

Sweeping her eyes around the small space she hears Brad's groans and spies a spare tube of lube.

Reaching over with her free hand as her second finger is buried deep within Becky, she stabs her hand up and Hans grabs the tube like a baton being passed.

Moving her mouth off Becky's plump pussy lips, Hans gets busy pouring lube over his cock. Greasing his own pole he bends over Becky and whispers a question.

"No!" she says, somewhat breathlessly, "I've never, ever had anything in my butt!"

Hans lets a small frown pucker his brow. "Hold still and stop squirming," he says, straightening.

"I don't know," she nearly caterwauls. "I—ah, oh my *gawd*," Becky says as Hans begins parking the very tip of his prick inside her untried assbud.

Pouring more lube over his shallow-pumping dick, Hans begins to stab forward, a fraction deeper inside her tight ass at a time.

Now that it's settled and their reluctant Becky seems to be playing along, Isabella begins to pump three fingers in her wet cunt.

Hans groans, clearly loving the *extra*-tight fit.

The real estate at the back end of Becky is narrow between pussy and ass.

Isabella doesn't mind, wanting to get her tongue in Becky's crack as Hans continues to plunder her ass, inch-by-unwilling-inch.

Isabella gives side-eye to Brad's plunder while her fingers and tongue alternate pumping and licking Becky.

Isabella determines Brad is definitely the more unwilling of the two.

Not that it's easy to tell. Lars is having none of that non-team player attitude, though. Currently, Brad is sinking to the root, dong implanted while bent way over—now giving Lars head.

Quite a bit of man-time considering young Brad had been *all about* the women.

Dara is equal opportunity and allowed Brad to have his pussy pie first—uncommon for Dara.

Maybe she was priming the pump, Isabella thinks, giving a snigger.

Just then, Zoe moves up behind Hans, who's just about stuffed his entire Johnson inside Becky.

Finally.

"Turn around is fair play," Zoe murmurs and swiping the half-gone lube tube off the control panel, she pours a generous dollop on her finger and running her index down the crack of Hans' ass, plunges the slick digit inside his rear entry.

"Ah!" Hans barks, halting his smooth assault on Becky for a moment as Zoe pushes her finger knuckle-deep.

Ass cheeks clenching, Isabella decides she'll be a multitasker and without further ado, reaches up with her non-buried hand and cups Hans' nutsack.

"My God," he breathes in soft Norwegian.

Isabella's eyes meet Zoe's.

With unspoken synchronicity, Zoe lifts another sexy dong, finger busy diving in and out between Hans' tight set of cheeks. This toy isn't hollowed-out like the one pretending to be a sleeve on top of the lever that's now rammed up Brad's ass.

Oh *no*. It's a pound of juicy fake love.

Zoe doesn't waste time and Isabella admires her enthusiasm.

As Hans continues to ream Becky's ass (and virgin ass or no, Becky's thick grunts of pleasure clearly spur him on), Zoe begins the lube and dip of the gigantic pleasure rod.

Hans stills, feeling something far thicker than a delicate female finger beginning to penetrate his back end.

"*Nei*," Hans says.

"*Ja*," Isabella returns smoothly. These men can't be part of the group and only participate the way *they* want.

Look at Becky? Isabella thinks, *she's gotten all her holes hammered and filled.*

Isabella frowns. Not the ass. That still needs a full offload.

Zoe better hurry things up.

Isabella keeps up her wet plunder of Becky then starts squeezing and fondling Hans' tight nutsack while Zoe begins grinding the toy in Hans' backend.

"That's too much," he says in strained Norwegian. Isabella had something that large and in charge at Dara's last soiree and Hans' will have to play too.

He's got a hole to fill.

"Ooooh, the manhole is a tight fit!" Zoe squeals in delight. Twirling the huge dong she begins to pump aggressively in Hans' assbud and in turn he pushes his impressive pale meat all the way into Becky getting owned ass.

Reaching around his front, Zoe drops another dollop of clear liquid on Hans' pumping rod and he smoothly pushes in and out of Becky as Zoe sets her own rhythm.

Isabella cranks down on his nuts just as Zoe slams the toy home, the fake nuts stick out at the end as Hans' blares a grunt above Becky and halts, spurting for all he's worth inside Becky as she moans beneath him.

Zoe slowly removes the dildo and Hans' exhale is pure

relief as Isabella removes her cum-drenched hand and tongue from Becky.

The two women stand, Zoe's tits swaying as she looks around for a handy resting spot for the used dong. Not seeing anything right away, Zoe shrugs and slaps it on the controls between a few buttons of importance.

"Hey, careful there," Hans mutters as he takes his sore ass away from a spread and used Becky, attempting to pull up his tight g-string underwear.

Becky sort of rolls over and gingerly sits on the co-pilot seat, cum leaking out of both holes and a fine bit lacing her lips.

"Wow," she says in a semi-daze.

Isabella likes the look of her just sitting there with nothing but the uniform vest on.

Lars glances Becky's way and sees that she's naked and spread with cum in all the right places.

Isabella doesn't need to be a brain surgeon to see his wheels turning.

Without so much as a word, he jerks his junk out of Brad's mouth and walks toward Becky.

"Well, it's time for Brad to earn his pay," Dara announces in a droll tone.

Isabella's eyes roam Brad, who appears to not be going anywhere fast, plugged as he is on the dong.

Zoe shrugs and with a small giggle, joins Dara where a small table has been inserted in front of the struggling Brad.

If he'd just stop squirming and start hopping up and down on the dong, a happy ending would be in sight.

But no matter. He has a mouth that needs a job.

Isabella and Zoe move in, slowly shedding their clothes.

Hans can recover and join them.

They're not near-through with Brad.

His widening eyes tell Isabella that he might be rethinking having interrupted them out in the first class cabin.

Rethinking it a lot.

24

DARA

BRAD NEEDS TO eat us girls out properly, Dara thinks with her typical determination.

She pauses her personal close-up inspection of his rigid cock, courtesy of her of course, to watch Lars move on to Becky and Hans appears as though he might need another magic blue pill.

Narrowing her eyes at Brad's mossy greens, Dara cards his short hair with nimble fingers, jerking up his head until they're eye level.

"It's time for you to do some up and down." Dara shifts her eyes to the impaled dong significantly.

"Here, Dara." Zoe helpfully hands her the lube.

Dara uncaps the top, pouring lube on Brad's soft prick.

Isabella begins to work Brad's cock.

Excellent. "Flip that lever down so he can bend over," Dara says.

Isabella's platinum brows draw together. "Won't that crash the plane?"

Legitimate point, Dara muses. Not wanting to explore the potential, Dara sighs, turning to Zoe.

"Zoe, please go around the back end there and take care of our Brad."

With a squeal of delight, Zoe scoots around Brad and positions herself behind him.

Dara releases Brad's hair, dragging a sturdy but small table directly in front of him.

Dara pops up on the glossy surface and wiggles her ass cheeks, gauging stability.

"That's not meant..." Hans begins in Norwegian.

Dara waves the comment away. Maybe it's a lunch table? And that's exactly what they'll use it for. *Eating.* Dara smirks. "Ready?"

Zoe's dark eyes meet hers from over Brad's shoulder.

His eyes widen, because clearly, the goal posts of his expectations have shifted.

"Born ready," Zoe quips.

Isabella lets off on her hand work for a moment as Dara situates herself just so. Hiking her skirt she moves it to around her waist, revealing her panty-less status.

As she'd anticipated, Brad's eyes dive to her bared goods.

At the precise moment Dara lays back, legs spread, Zoe grabs ahold of the huge dong and gently shoves Brad forward.

His palms smack the sides of the small wood table Dara's lying on and the furniture shudders under his abrupt touch.

Dara grips the edges with her fingertips. "You partake of the pussy buffet; Zoe and Isabella will take care of the rest."

"That, you're—" Brad's eyes take in her spread parts.

Oh this is delightful, she thinks, giving Brad a coy glance from beneath her eyelashes. She loves watching the internal struggle of a new player.

"I know," Dara cuts him off, winking at Zoe who dumps

Brad forward a bit more, cleverly removing his ass by default from the sock of the dong covering the pilots' lever.

"Oops!" Zoe says with alarm.

"That... *shit!*" Hans says as the plane's nose takes a bit of a sharp dip.

Hans' dangle flies around as he rushes to the lever, expertly moving it back into position.

He and Lars exchange a slightly frantic look.

But jerk of the plane rolled Dara off the table and landed her directly on her ass in a most unflattering way. "Dammit," she says, moving to her hands and knees, feeling around her derrière to ascertain damage. Dara scoots between Brad's arms and clambers up on the table again.

Brad says, "I didn't sign up for this."

"When you say yes to Dara, it's actually a 'yes' to *everything*," Isabella explains as though to a four-year old.

Dara adores Isabella's insights, though a potential plane crash could get a bit sticky.

There's a frantic knock at the cockpit door and Dara rolls her eyes. Just when she was going to get some attention.

Becky trots the short distance (apparently revived enough to walk, though it is a bit slower than when they began) and slides the lock aside, peeking as she hides her lower half behind the door.

Isabella grins, dropping Brad's softened erection in favor of something else.

Dara watches with interest.

"What in the blue hell is going on with the plane?" asks a masculine voice from right outside the door.

Oooh, a male flight attendant, maybe another rooster could join them inside the chicken coop.

One who clearly thinks he can demand answers.

Dara loves to shut down that line of thinking in short order.

"Isabella," Zoe whisper-hisses.

Bella smiles, just an upturn of lips, really, walking swiftly to the door. Without any coaching, she flings the door wide, baring the inside of the cockpit.

A handsome, somewhat lean male flight attendant looks inside at all the half-naked fun and gasps when a disheveled Becky, wearing only one piece of her original uniform, is revealed before him in mainly naked glory.

"What's going on here?" he asks rhetorically while those smoky light eyes dart knowingly around the scene.

Well... everything, Dara thinks. *He's wearing a tie*, she notes a millisecond before Bella uses the neck ornament as a handle, dragging him within the already-tight space and firmly closing the narrow cockpit door behind him.

"What the...!"

Lovely.

With an efficient slide, the cockpit lock is reengaged and Isabella spins the slightly dazed... Dara sweeps his nameplate from her position, *Alex* and relishes that he appears to be within her favorite age group.

Young.

Dara has standards. Too young and they're consumed about the size of their equipment. However, just a tad older and they're only worried about getting their equipment where it belongs.

Where Dara tells them.

Isabella has twirled and slammed a bewildered Alex against the door.

"Isn't he dee-*lish*!" Zoe says, performing an amazing leprechaun hop with zero room.

"Zoe," Dara admonishes.

"I know, I know—*Brad.*" She cocks her head, reluctantly turning away from the new rooster, Alex.

Yes, Brad. *Cock-a-doodle-do.*

Dara dismisses Alex (for the moment) and shifts her attention to Brad. A light sweat glistens above his upper lip and with a deep sigh of relief, Zoe presses his face near Dara's soaked aroused snatch.

His lips move right to her clit and Dara groans, spreading her legs wider for easier access.

Brad's empty ass is wide open for more fun and Zoe industriously grabs yet another handy dong. With practiced hands, unloads the lube on its length, lining the tip up with Brad's tender assbud.

"Careful," Dara says, thinking Brad might give her a reactive nip on her delicate lower lips.

"Huh?" Brad lifts his head just as Zoe begins to push the new dong within his empty needy hole.

"Hey," he chimes with much less vigor than with the sleeve dong.

They all come around eventually.

Zoe begins to move the dong, just a light back and forth shove in the first third of his assbud. "Brad, get back to business," Dara instructs, giving a "can't miss it" point of her black, french-tipped nail directly at her honeypot.

And as a handy contingency, Dara threads her fingers through his hair, dumping his face right in the center of her pussy.

"Lick me and finger fuck me," Dara commands.

Brad's tongue sweeps her, entrance to clit, spending extra time on her tight teeny bundle of nerves. When his fat, long finger finds her pussy and begins to dive into her wetness Dara throws her head back, adding her other hand to plummet through his locks and push his face deeper into her wet heat.

"Zoe!" Dara calls out in a hoarse shout.

Without missing a beat, Zoe begins to alternately lube and shove the new dong with deep, penetrating thrusts.

Brad's body starts to rock with the motion of getting his ass owned, moaning against Dara's soaked core as he fucks her hard with two fingers.

Dara licks her lips. "Oh this is good."

"I'm out of here," Alex states, eyes latched onto the sight of the dong train with a caboose of pussy clean up.

"Be reasonable, Alex," Dara hears Lars say, deeming him a team player.

"Just because you're the pilots of this aircraft doesn't give you the right to do whatever bullshit you want by tossing the controls to autopilot."

Bossy. Dara's eyes fling open, drilling Alex to the spot. "You are *not* going to ruin my fun, Alex." She loops Hans and Becky with a severe eye sweep.

"I didn't—I don't want," Alex's light gray eyes look around the interior cockpit as though for support, "this."

"It's not about what you want, Alex," Dara clarifies with a breathy catch in her voice because just at that precise moment, Brad decides to level-up with the addition of a new finger.

"Of course it is," Alex says, moving to the door.

That doesn't work, really—because lovely Bella blocks the way.

By this time, she's shucked the cream-colored slacks, Dara notices from her upside down position (now entirely too warm for their sub-tropical destination) and stands in an impressive barely-there nude g-string and understated high heels. Bella's tall to begin with, hailing from Scandinavia and now she towers over dishrag Alex, who Dara is beginning to wonder will actually join in the fun. "You need to rethink your priorities of being part of the group, Alex."

"Yes," Hans adds quickly, attempting to tuck his uncooperative fleshen sword of a dick back within the confines of his underwear.

Finally giving up, he strides the short distance to Alex's position.

Alex, for his part, can't take his eyes from Hans' bobbing cock. Adam's apple giving a hard plow up and down he says, "What am I supposed to do with the passengers?"

Ah. Not so reluctant after all.

Hans says, "Isn't Melody and Shelby outside taking care of them?"

Alex shrugs. "I was supposed to let the passengers know what the hell happened with the plane—we don't want mass hysteria."

Dara likes the *mass* part.

Just then Brad does a little suck and twirl with his tongue on her clit and she blows, deep pulses wracking her body as Brad keeps up the relentless rhythm to match what Zoe's doing with his ass.

Dara floats back to herself in pieces of exquisite ecstasy, finally coming back to the conversation that has all-but-stopped.

Alex's eyes are all for Dara. "If I stay can I get some of that." Alex says, clearly having abandoned the idea of doing his job. At least, the one where he gets paid, if his eyes latched onto her throbbing cunt are any indicator.

Dara gives a satisfied smile as her eyes roam the room and she comes up with Becky and Isabella half-clothed and realizes Zoe and Isabella are practically daisy-fresh.

Time to amend that.

"Boys." Hans and Lars come to attention.

"It's time to break in the new guy."

Dara adores watching Alex's face as his expression tells the war of what he'll decide.

Is he going to stay and take his chances?

Or will he trudge back out to serve coffee to the disgruntled frequent fliers.

25

ISABELLA

THE COCKPIT DOOR is engaged. Alex isn't going anywhere. Let him believe the fantasy of escape.

Isabella didn't drop her merino wool drawers for nothing. She has expectations.

Dara didn't have the final exam like she'd promised and Isabella is slightly miffed about that even though she assured Isabella there would be an exam upon arrival. And Isabella has she received any fun.

Becky received *lots* of fun. But she and Zoe, the traveling companions, have just confined whoever needed to receive.

Like Alex.

Isabella looks over the dull tool before her and does concede Brad is even more of one. Nonetheless, who says the swinging dicks have to be clever?

Certainly not her. Isabella gives a stern glance at the pilots, nearly twins with their fair good looks and tall builds.

"Bring him into the fold, I guess," Isabella says in Norwegian.

Zoe stomps a foot. "I hate that when you switch languages, I don't know what's going on."

"We would rather not prepare Alex for our adventures too much," Isabella admits.

"Oh," Zoe says in a small voice, continuing to fuck the hapless Brad out of corn cob.

All right, Isabella thinks, *I'll take pity on Brad.*

Isabella walks away from Alex, already dismissing his participation and takes ahold of Brad's junk once again.

With a steady hand, Isabella goes back to working the hardening length.

Dara slides from the tiny table where she'd got her pussy lapped and slides beneath Brad.

"Let me just..." Dara begins contemplatively.

"Argh!" Brad yells into the space.

"Whaaaaat?" Dara asks innocently.

Dara does nothing innocent, Isabella thinks, gaze shifting to what her busy hands are employing.

Dara is running her finger at that line of flesh that runs from asshole to nutsack and squeezing Brad's testies.

Ah.

This works in tandem with what Isabella does. Except... Isabella bends over and begins sucking off Brad as she uses her hand just ahead of her lip-latch.

"Oh my God!" Brad screams, hips thrusting forward as her thumb feels the sensation of his dick beginning to throb as his cum sweeps from his balls to the tip of his dick.

Removing his hands from the table he fists Isabella's hair and brings her face to the root of his cock, helplessly lifting his hips as he releases his hot load inside her mouth.

For her part, Isabella takes it all, swallowing the entire steaming stream of seed to the very last excellent drop.

Yum, she thinks, raising her head as Brad sags from exhaustion.

Dara grins, easily coming to a standing position as Zoe

removes the dong with a slow, expert twist and tosses the used appendage to join the others.

"That's not going to work," Lars comments thoughtfully, eyeing up the growing pile of dongs now sticking to the buttons and knobs.

"It works fine. Let maintenance sort that," Dara says with her favorite dismissive wave.

"There might be negative repercussions to all that," Hans comments darkly.

Dara gives him her full attention. "Then chuck me under the bus, Hans. We're having fun here. That is," her brows pluck into a frown, "until you began worrying about consequences."

"Fuck that," Zoe says decisively.

"Dara, darling," Hans begins.

She shakes her head, dark auburn locks swirling across the tops of her demi-cups. "We have Alex now who has impeccable timing, given Brad," Dara pats Brad's head as he's now collapsed into the pilots' chair, where lube, cum and sweat now decorate the seat alongside his naked butt cheeks, "needs a brief hiatus."

Brad dumps his head against the headrest. "Hell yeah."

Dara graces him with a benign smile then shifts her attention to the vikings.

Alex's eyes continue to widen, but like many before him, Isabella believes he will eventually be a Dara fan.

His tongue runs the length of his bottom lip. "I just want at that twat," he says, pointing vaguely at Dara, or her pretty pussy.

Dara pouts, hands to hips. "I'd thought you might be more advanced, Alex."

"Advanced?" His head jerks back, clearly in a gesture of

insult or annoyance. "What does that mean—I can't get it on?"

Alex huffs and begins jerking down his pants in an unsexy and economical disrobing. "See," he says, sweeping his hand at his now-erect penis that supports the tails of his button-down shirt in a comical tent at the tip.

Oh dear, Isabella thinks, looking to Dara and Zoe.

Zoe smiles knowingly.

"All right. Manner training is forthcoming you uncouth young man," Dara says.

Hans and Lars back away, clearly having gone through a minor course themselves and not wanting a refresher.

"Zoe," Dara says commandingly.

Zoe skedaddles around Brad and chases after Dara, who's making her deliberate way to Alex. "Goody," Zoe says under her breath, easily reaches Isabella.

The pair of woman close in on Alex.

"I just want the redhead," Alex says, running his eyes over gorgeous Zoe and giving a sniff.

Zoe grunts in the background and Isabella can admit she feels slighted herself. *Dara won't let that play out,* Isabella decides a moment before Dara confirms with, "The 'redhead' calls the shots."

He reaches out and plucks a breast from her swimmingly blue bra and Dara puts her hand on his bare erect length, a dark crimson eyebrow arching prettily as they stare each other down.

"Fuck, you get *after* shit," Alex announces after seconds have pounded by. Squeezing the globe of her breast, the flesh oozes out from his palm and he pauses to admire it.

Dara cups his nuts and lets Alex have a squeeze that looks to Isabella like it rides the edge of pain.

His eyes tighten. "I don't want any cock love from those dongs in my ass," Alex says.

"Okay," Dara agrees breezily, a benign smile stretching her full lips.

That's when Isabella knows for a concrete certainty that Alex will get plenty up his ass.

"Dara," Hans calls out softly.

"Yes?" Dara says, still rhythmically squeezing Alex's nuts.

"Autopilot must eventually disengage for us to land."

"Dammit," Dara mutters. "Okay—we don't have all day. Let's get down to business."

"Great," Alex enthuses, "lie down and spread those long legs. I'll bury my tool and make you come."

"Yes, well," Dara traces a long nail down the center of his chest and gooseflesh follows the gesture like a wake after a boat, "that's lovely, but for now I'd like you to get on your hands and knees."

He shakes his head.

Dara lifts a leg and without a thought, Isabella grabs the spot directly underneath her bent knee, holding the leg up.

Alex's eyes latch on to her glistening, glossy labia.

He swallows. "Okay."

"Good boy." Dara points at the limited cockpit floor space and after a heartbeat's hesitation, Alex sinks to the ground.

The instant he's on the ground everyone crowds around (even the recovered Hans, though Brad still warms the pilot's seat).

"I want to make him pay for his comments," Zoe says, miffed.

Isabella agrees.

Swiftly, Lars plucks his uniform pants from the back of the co-pilot seat.

"No," Becky speaks for the first time since Alex entered, "I have just the thing."

"Hold your horses," Dara says and lowers herself she expertly shimmies into position beneath Alex.

"I can't wait to fuck that redhead pussy," Alex says.

Zoe glowers.

Dara gives a minute shake of her head as though telling Zoe *quiet*, spreading all that admired red hair around her with the gesture.

"I can't dig in when your legs are closed," Alex says in a growl above her.

Dara purses her lips, then carefully uses her heels to shove herself deeper into the space and further away from the door, thereby making more room behind Alex then spreads her legs.

Isabella swiftly puts the plan's pieces together.

Smiling, she moves up behind Alex, whose eyes are all for Dara's face.

"Bash away," Dara incites, giving a final calculating look at Becky, Isabella and Zoe.

"He's always been an asshole," Becky mutters for the girls to hear.

Zoe smirks, slapping another dildo from the insatiable supply into Becky's palm.

The young woman's eyes widen.

"No, no, that's not how things are done," Hans says, moving behind Alex who has started to sink his cock inside Dara.

"Oh man, this is so hot, she's as tight and slick as I thought she'd be," Alex groans, hips leaping forward to sink more meat inside Dara, who hikes her hips up to aggressively meets his strokes.

Dara looks up at Hans and winks.

Hans nods, moving into position.

Isabella taps a nail at her chin. *She* wants a fucking. And the thought of Alex getting thoroughly owned while it's happening?

Awesome.

Alex enthusiastically grinds forward and Zoe pours the lube vertically down his ass crack.

He stills, half-buried within Dara. "What. The. Hell?"

It's an absolute repeat of Brad.

But then Alex whips his butt up and Dara scoots from beneath him and Isabella doesn't waste any time, taking her place.

"Hey!" Alex begins

But Zoe's there, taking care of his spouting mouth by shoving a dong in it like a ball-gag.

Meanwhile, Hans gets busy with Alex's back end, which appears to be on the menu for Mr. Belligerent.

Grabbing his ass, Isabella draws him down as Hans begins to dip his wick.

"Oh god," Alex says from around the stuffed dong.

Isabella is ready, her pussy is engorged and plump from watching and being a part of all the fun, but now she *finally* gets a prick.

Clearly Alex isn't as fussy about what girl he wanted because Isabella gets into place and Hans, planting his hands pushup style alongside Alex's shoulders, dives inside his spread ass cheeks.

"Ah," comes Alex's muffled shout.

The sensation of him plowing forward is like being speared. Isabella arches her back, taking the combined weight of the men and feeling Alex's long shlong kiss her womb.

She moans, writhing beneath Alex but wanting even more cock. As if on erotic cue, Lars sinks to his knees directly in front of Alex.

Isabella doesn't think that plan is physically possible, even if a contortionist wanted it.

Then he does it. Alex turns his head to the side, pumping deeply inside her as Lars removes the dong Zoe parked in there and replaces it with his own prick inside Alex's wet mouth.

"Wow," Zoe and Becky say simultaneously.

Orgasm is too close for Isabella to notice anything except the shadow of the cock above her face, fucking Alex's mouth and the delicious extra weight of Hans pumping his ass.

With another thrust Isabella's pussy blows up, squeezing and releasing Alex's cock.

She mewls below him, her pussy pulsing like a freight train.

"Nicely played, Hans," Dara says as the tall man stiffens above Alex, clearly giving him both barrels of cum.

Not to be outdone, Lars gives a muffled groan and with soft fast pumps, unleashes his load inside Alex's mouth.

The gush of Alex's cum filling Isabella is sweet consolation for the attention-deprived flight.

In the future, she might have to bring someone along for them. Or several someones.

Lars and Hans remove their beef fuel injectors from Alex and he sort of rolls off Isabella with a gasp, flopping onto his back.

"Well, that was distracting," Dara says then turns,

pulling Becky in tight and giving her a breath-stealing french kiss.

When Dara pulls away, Becky appears slightly stunned and says, "An unforgettable first class passenger manifest."

"No more autopilot, Dara."

Dara tries not pouting at Lars and misses the mark by a smidge.

Isabella stands, visually hunting around for her pants, deciding they're too warm and scoops her panties off the cupped window ledge within the cockpit.

Alex is still laid out flat on the floor.

Dara gifts him with a tiny scowl. "Get up now, the vikings need the controls back."

Everyone looks at the nasty stack of dongs hovering above essential controls.

"Alex can hang around if he promises to take more of what he's already received – later," Lars says casually.

"I can't *take* any more," Brad pipes in for the first time.

Zoe barks out a laugh. "Yeah, you got your pipes reamed."

"That's an interesting way of putting it," Isabella remarks, though she thinks Brad might not be a return player. She looks over his exhausted slouch within the pilot's chair where a passable attempt has been made at reclothing himself.

Definitely not.

Dara must have the same leanings as she tears him from the chair by his elbow. "Shoo."

Brad's dark eyebrows slowly rise. "Shoo?" he asks incredulously.

Dara nods. "Why yes, if the vikings can bring the action and a young mouthy thing like yourself is whining about being tired? No."

"Just no," Zoe says, crossing her arms beneath her luscious rack.

Becky nods, disengaging the lock and stepping away from the door.

"Am I being dismissed?" Brad asks, eyes traveling the assorted faces.

"Seems that way, dolt," Alex says from the floor and crosses his legs at the ankle.

Bending over, Zoe holds up a palm and Alex slaps her palm with a half-hearted high five.

He might do, Isabella thinks with mild surprise as Alex seemed so unrefined on first blush.

"I'll stick around," Alex comments as Brad stalks from the cockpit.

"I don't like his attitude," Lars remarks, using a wipe to clean up the seat and settles in. His tie is long gone and his pilot wings are askew.

"Ja," Hans agrees, doing his own sterilization of his seat and sits as well.

"Ladies," Hans says.

"Oh poo," Dara says, collecting her clothes and sliding everything back into place.

Isabella, Zoe and Becky do the same.

"Well damn," Zoe says, eyeballing the cockpit.

"There's always more flights," Lars says.

"Yes," Dara says, leaning over Lars' shoulder and kissing his cheek.

The women step over Alex, who's claimed the middle of the floor and Dara gives a teeny snort at the sight.

Becky has put on her vest inside out and Isabella decides that's proof of a good time.

They leave the cockpit with Becky following and take their respective seats.

The women sit quietly for a moment, clearly reflecting on the past couple of hours of fun when and unwelcome voice says, "You ladies going to get your tacos stuffed?"

Dara sits up and turns toward the intruder on their ruminating.

Brad smirks.

It appears Brad has rested up from everything, though the snarky attitude remains.

Dara is never overwhelmed by anything. She volleys a smirk right back. "Not by you."

Brad glares at her and with a smooth pivot, Dara turns back to face forward in her seat, leaning her head against the back of the seat.

Dara closes her eyes to take a catnap.

After all, there's an entire new country to scour for diversions once they arrive.

THE END

Read where it all began:
https://books2read.com/DARA1-8-210424

☞ *Your words are powerful.* If you liked this sexy compilation of hot stories, keep me writing by posting your star rating/thoughts:
https://books2read.com/DARAcontinuation-1-5-220123
and help another reader discover a new author. ***Thank you!***

Love Dara? *Read on for Bonus chapters....*

26
BONUS CH. 1

I looked at the clock, *yet again*... and knew that if my boss caught me I'd be toast. Safe in my cubicle, I swung my gaze away from the the dreaded time and looked for Michelle. She'd be hanging by the cooler, *which she was*.

Michelle caught me looking and lifted her chin up in greeting and grinned. She knew what I was about. It was all about getting out of here and doing something for ourselves. It had been a Long-Damn-Week and I was going to let my hair down and have some fun.

Michelle wrapped up her conversation with one of the petty chicks that lounged all day while we picked up the slack.

As Michelle walked toward me, I thought that maybe we wouldn't have to change: pencil skirts, thigh high stockings, stacked heels and blouses that yoked just where they should be to look sexy, nothing too much.

Michelle stood in front of me, tapping a foot. "Watching the time won't help it go faster."

"Yes, I know, but I feel like the day should have ended already."

"I've got an idea, let's go to Spinners tonight," she nearly squealed in delight. I wasn't feelin' the love on that place. It was always packed with a rough crowd and you had to beat the guys off with a bat.

Michelle saw my expression and started to wheedle immediately, "Listen, give it a half hour and if it's super-lame, we'll just bail and go somewhere else. Like that brewery place... what's it's name?"

"Talbot's," I replied absently.

She snapped her fingers. "That's it!"

"Listen," she leaned forward and our hair mingled together, "that new gal... with the red hair..."

"Molly?" I said, automatically looking around for her.

"Yeah," she waved her hand, dismissing the name. "She was talking about that piece of creepy news that's been circulating today."

I looked at her blankly.

"Oh for shit's sake, Rachel! Don't you pay attention to anything?"

"Not really," I said noncommittally. My life was beyond boring right now. I worked here, hung out with Michelle, worked out, read, fed my cat. I was dying for some Excitement. *Dying*. But the news wasn't going to deliver. Excitement... no way.

"You're hopeless! Anyway," she sounded the syllables out slowly, "there's been another killing. Another bleed-out."

That got my attention.

It had been almost a month since the first murder and they still hadn't found the killer.

Then there were the rapes.

Somehow, it was all connected. Men were killed and drained dry of their blood and if there were women with them, they were raped.

But none of the women could remember the attack or their attacker.

Our gazes locked. "So... they found another body. Two, actually." Michelle said ominously, waggling two fingers.

Great. Just when I thought we could flounce around for the weekend. Talk about a wet blanket.

"Maybe... we shouldn't go to Spinners then. I mean, if it's not safe."

"Eff-that, you're going! I just wanted to spread the gory gossip."

"That's kinda sick, you know."

Michelle nodded vigorously, she knew.

I sighed. There was no getting out of it once Michelle had her mind set. And, in my soul... if I didn't get a break from this job and do something out-of-body, I'd scream.

"I gotcha talked right into it, don't I?" Her eyes sparkled.

"I guess but, we need to be careful, especially now," I said in a conspirator's whisper.

"Hell, I'm more worried about the regular guys."

"Were the women... you know, was there blood... there?" I asked.

She spun back around, her skirt twirling a little with the motion. "That's the major weird thing, they had all been bitten, but still had their blood. Only a pint gone."

Well, wasn't that just *comforting*.

Michelle winked as she sauntered off, hips swaying. "Pick ya up at seven sharp."

She didn't wait for me to respond. Michelle knew she had me, hook, line and sinker.

I gathered up all my stuff, slipped my heels back on my feet and headed for the door.

Unfortunately, my dragon lady of a boss was blocking my way.

"Miss Collins, I see you're ready to leave." She looked at her behemoth of a wristwatch. "Two minutes after five." She raised a humongous unibrow at me and I stifled a giggle. It was hard to be pissed at her when she looked so ridiculous.

Almost.

"Yes. That's traditionally when the work day ends for us here, Ms. Hogan," I replied, thinking with mild irritation that Hogan had me by the short hairs. She knew I needed the job, she couldn't lambast me for leaving when the work day was through, technically. But... she liked to make me feel *diminished* for leaving so close to the chiming of the clock.

Hogan looked me over from head to toe, taking in my long black hair, so deep a black it had blue highlights in the right light. My eyes were a pale blue, I was shapely but not skinny, and on the tall side. I didn't consider myself a hot number but I held my own. Hogan, on the other hand looked like she was always trolling for a new bridge.

I had discreetly pressed my elbow into the elevator button and it dinged just as she opened her mouth to mention something else equally unimportant, her jowls swinging as she popped her mouth open then closed it again.

I felt my escape portal open at my back and walked backwards into its gaping mouth, never more glad to be out of mortar range of the enraged cow, aka my boss.

She glowered at me, starting to waddle forward and I blurted out, "Have a great weekend!" The door swept closed in front of me.

I did a mental forehead-wipe. Thank God I was out of

there.

As the elevator descended I prepared myself for the onslaught of cold weather, my car would need at least five minutes to heat up. The days were long here in the north and heating my car in the underground parking garage was just part of what we did in Alaska.

The elevator doors hissed apart and the cold air swept into the tight space, momentarily stealing my breath. I huddled my full length coat around myself, silently wishing the car was already warm. I rushed out of the elevator's cocoon of heat, my heels making clicking sounds on the concrete as I made my way to my car. If you could call it that.

As I approached I knew my car stood out, it was a Smart Car and Michelle liked to tease and say it was a toaster that I drove, not a real car. I smiled, she had me there.

I fumbled with my keys, finally yanking my glove off with my teeth, groaning as the cold air assaulted my fingertips, making them instantly numb.

"Hey, Rachel,"

I dropped my keys on the ground, spinning, my hand to my heart.

It was Erik, a guy from work. My shoulders slumped in relief. He scared the shit out of me.

"Scare you?" he smiled.

I smiled back tentatively. He had really been pursuing me and I wasn't that interested. I couldn't put my finger on it exactly but there was just something *off* about him.

Erik approached me and I stiffened a little, but he bent over, jerking the keys off the ground and put a finger through the loop of my key fob and hung them off his finger in front of my nose.

I tried to snatch them and he yanked them just out of

reach.

"Meet me for dinner," he stated, his eyes steady on my face, disconcerting.

"Ah... Michelle and I are going out tonight," I said, trying to distract him.

"Rain check?" he pressed, never stopping his eye contact. I was starting to get nervous.

Damn.

I resisted the supreme urge to look around, seeing if there was anyone else. But there wasn't. I could feel the absence of others. I sure wasn't short on woman's intuition. *Just another creepy service we offer*, I thought, getting the heebie-jeebies.

I closed my coat tighter around me and his eyes tracked the movement, a smile spreading on his face. "I'll let you go, I know you have plans." But his face told another tale. I didn't think he'd forget my rebuff anytime soon.

I held my hands out and I was happy to notice that they weren't shaking. He'd really put me in a creeped out mood and I wasn't happy about it.

He dropped the keys into my cupped hands and smiled again, tipping an imaginary hat.

I turned after his back was to me and stabbed the key into the lock, opening the door in one movement I slid behind the wheel, slapping the flat of my palm on the lock after it closed. I heard the simultaneous click in the silence of the car and let the breath out I didn't realize I'd been holding.

Holy-hell.

I turned on the car and stewed for the five minutes, all the while wishing I could have driven off.

That encounter with Erik had put a bad taste in my mouth. Like diet pop, but somehow worse.

I pulled out of the bowels of the building, the night as black as when the day started. I entered traffic and began the drive to my condo, almost in the heart of downtown.

I couldn't wait to be home.

I threw my lights on, and glancing right then left I was so startled that I almost let my foot off the brake into opposing traffic.

Erik sat behind the wheel of his car. He'd been sitting there the entire time... waiting for me.

I gunned it at the first hole in traffic that appeared. What a whacko!

I'd have to tell Michelle he was a nut-job. She'd have him cracked in no time.

~

I HAD my head thrown back and my lips parted, the last swipe of mascara almost perfect... there! I stood back and looked at my reflection: definitely not work attire. I was so glad I made the decision to not perk up the whole mess with just a new top. Michelle probably would have flogged me if I had anyway. She'd be dressed-to-kill (as usual). I needed to make an effort. Sometimes, I wondered why I bothered. Michelle would go, shine, get picked-up, bang some anonymous stud in the bathroom or wherever, and I would sip my drink wishing I could go home and curl up with a book. I sighed. That's okay. She was... my vicarious slutty friend. And I loved her.

I grabbed my vanilla body spray and squirted a last dab. If I ended up dancing a lot, I'd be glad I wore it. It was frigid outside but once we were inside Spinners, with all the bodies packed in there, it'd be a different story.

I heard the doorknob jiggle and caught sight of Michelle

coming through the doorway looking delectable in her slut suit. She twirled for me so I could get the full effect.

"That should be illegal!" I nearly screamed. She had a micro-mini on that was two part: it cupped her ass and was barely legal (skimming the indecent exposure laws by a millimeter). It was hot pink, setting off her platinum hair to perfection. She "helped" the color of said hair, but not by a lot. Michelle was a rare thing up here in the frozen north and I was betting that it was her coloring that got her so much attention, and the boobs... and the outfits. And, and....

I smiled as she circled me like a shark, gauging my potential for Attracting the Opposite Sex.

"I don't know... is this the shortest skirt you have?" Her brows closed the distance between her eyes.

I self-consciously ran my hand over my short black skirt, it barely covered the lace of my thigh-highs... a gorgeous pair that I had splurged on from Italy.

"Yeah, I can't go much shorter without the lace tops showing."

Michelle gave me a blank look. "Seriously, that's part of the allure."

"Ah... no. I say let them guess. It *is* underwear after all."

"I say show it!" Michelle said.

"Mystery," I replied.

She threw her hand up. "Whatever, I give up. At least you did right by the top."

I had almost not worn it, it was a scorching crimson and showed off my raven hair, my eyes stranded like startled jewels in my pale face. It left my arms bare and was tucked inside the skirt.

Michelle allowed her glance to linger a moment longer on my outfit, then shook her head as we walked out. I gave a quick pet to Caesar the cat and waltzed out.

BONUS CH. 2

Spinners was packed as usual and we jockeyed for position, awkwardly elbowing everyone without trying to maim people. It was always this way.

I couldn't believe our luck! I spied a couple of bar stools and we raced over there to stake our claim before they were snatched up. We perched our butts on the stools, aimlessly looking around at the bodies packed together, dancing the night away. I noticed they had already opened all the windows, allowing the sub-twenty degree air in. It didn't matter, it felt like a balmy eighty where we sat.

The bartender got our drinks. I sipped on a Blue Hawaiian and Michelle had Sex on the Beach (of course). She swung her leg back and forth and I was getting a spot-on flash of bright red panties... and so were a bunch of guys, judging from the expression of the gaggle of hunks sitting across from us.

"So what happened with Erik?"

"Yeah!" I yelled to be heard over the din. "He did this weird thing with my keys..." and I told her the whole thing.

Michelle leaned forward to catch everything because the noise was swallowing my words.

She leaned back against the bar, her elbows flung back and her wrists dangling off the edge, looking thoughtful. For Michelle that meant she was quiet for more than one minute.

Finally she said, "Yeah, you want to stay away from him. I hear he went out with some girl and date-raped her."

Perfect, I thought. That'd kinda been the vibe I was getting off him. Wasn't sure that confirmation was the greatest thing in this case, after all, I worked with the weirdo.

Wonderful.

I was momentarily distracted when two of the cute guys across the way sidled over to us. The one on the right was almost as blonde as Michelle but that's where the similarity ended. He was a head taller than her with brown eyes and a face that had seen acne in its youth. I guess he was ruggedly handsome. He spent time in the gym; it was in the set of his shoulders, the way he moved... like he had purpose.

Tonight his purpose was Michelle.

His eyes never left the foot that swung, traveling up to the apex of what the skirt almost showed. He looked like a dog ready to mount a bitch. It did something for her because her foot stopped swinging and she gave him the come hither look.

The night was Going According to Plan.

"Want to dance, cutie-pie?" she asked, batting her eyelashes. He all but panted while I rolled my eyes in my head. I just couldn't do it. It's not that I'd never had sex. Casual just wasn't a main entree. I dreamed that there was someone for me in my future. Someone that I could share something with. I felt almost like... almost like I was waiting.

Michelle argued there was plenty to be shared. She was into sharing.

Generous Michelle.

I watched her on the dance floor, plastered to Rugged, grinding for all she was worth, he was all over her and she was loving it.

I took my eyes off them and looked at the guy in front of me. He was way cuter than Rugged. He had the enigmatic *something* that made a girl want to get a little closer.

So I did.

"Do you want to dance?" he asked.

I nodded. He held out his hand, which was big I noticed. I tried not to think about how it would feel to have those hands roaming over my body but couldn't quite do it. He took me up against him and I molded against his torso. As those hands came to rest on the small of my back, the heat from them warmed me. He looked into my eyes and they held a promise of a fun night... if that's what I wanted. I didn't grind against him but I could feel that he was happy to be there. He smiled at me, knowing I was aware of his arousal.

He clutched me tighter and lowered his face next to mine and whispered, "Your friend's gone." Now he was kissing my neck.

Unease crept its way along my body. Usually Michelle gave me some kind of signal or something. I looked around for her trying not to feel frantic.

"Where did they go?" I semi-shouted at him.

"Outside!" He inclined his head in the direction of the door.

"You want to go find them?" he asked, his fingers already twining in mine.

I looked down at our clasped hands and that feeling of

unease bloomed in me again. I couldn't shake it. I understood on some level that I was just getting residual anxiety from the strange encounter with Erik and letting that cloud my thinking. I wasn't going to take it out on this guy.

"Yeah, let's find them," I said decisively.

I should have listened to that voice inside my head.

Reapers is also available in paperback!

ACKNOWLEDGMENTS

I published both *The Druid and Death Series*, in 2011 with the encouragement of my husband, and continued because of you, my Reader. Your faithfulness, through comments, suggestions, spreading the word and ultimately purchasing my work with your hard-earned money gave me the incentive, means and inspiration to continue.

There are no words that are sufficiently adequate to express my thankfulness for your support.

I truly feel connected to my readers. It is obvious to me, but I'll say the words anyway for clarity: a written work is just words on pages if they are not read by my readers. As I write this I get a lump in my throat; your enjoyment of my work affects me that deeply.

You guys are the greatest, each and every one of ya~

Tamara
   xoxo

   You, my reader.
   My husband, who is my biggest fan.
Cameren, without who, there would be no books.

ABOUT THE AUTHOR

www.tamararoseblodgett.com

<u>Tamara Rose Blodgett</u>: happily married mother of four sons. Dark thriller writer. Reader. Dreamer. Beachcombing slave. Tie dye zealot. Coffee addict. Digs music.

She is also the *New York Times* bestselling author of <u>*A Terrible Love*</u>, written under the pen name, Marata Eros, and 70 other novels. Other bestseller accolades include her #1 bestselling **TOKEN** (dark romance), **DRUID** (dark PNR erotica), **ROAD KILL MC** (thriller/top 100) **DEATH** (sci-fi dark fantasy) series. Tamara writes a variety of dark fiction in the genres: erotica, fantasy, horror, romance, sci-fi, suspense and thriller. She splits her time between the

Pacific NW and Mazatlán Mexico, spending time with family, friends and a pair of disrespectful dogs.

To be the first to hear about new releases and bargains—from Tamara Rose Blodgett/Marata Eros—sign up below to be on my VIP List. (I swear I won't spam or share your email with anyone!)

SIGN UP TO BE ON THE **MARATA EROS** VIP LIST

https://tinyurl.com/SubscribeMarataEros-News

SIGN UP TO BE ON THE **TAMARA ROSE BLODGETT** VIP LIST https://tinyurl.com/SubscribeTRB-News

Connect with Tamara:

Gettr

Clapper

MeWe

https://rumble.com/c/TamaraRoseBlodgett

Website:

www.tamararoseblodgett.com

Follow Marata Eros on Bookbub:

https://www.bookbub.com/profile/marata-eros

Follow Tamara Rose Blodgett on Bookbub:

https://www.bookbub.com/authors/tamara-rose-blodgett

ALSO BY MARATA EROS

♥ Read more titles from this author ♥

A Terrible Love (NYT & USA Today bestseller)

The Reflective – REFLECTION

Punished – ALPHA CLAIM

Death Whispers – DEATH

The Pearl Savage - SAVAGE

Blood Singers – BLOOD

Noose – ROAD KILL MC

Provocation – TOKEN

Ember – SIREN

Brolach – DEMON

Reapers - DRUID

Club Alpha – BILLIONAIRE'S GAME TRILOGY

Dara Nichols Volume 1 – DARA NICHOLS (18+)

Her

Through Dark Glass

The Fifth Wife (written with NYT bestseller Emily Goodwin)

A Brutal Tenderness

The Darkest Joy

DARA NICHOLS SERIES 1-5
A Dara Nichols World Novelette Compilation
Volume 2

New York Times BESTSELLER
MARATA EROS

ISBN: 9798418889591
Copyright © 2021-22 by Marata Eros
All rights reserved.No part of this book may be reproduced in any form or by any electronic or mechanical means, including information storage and retrieval systems, without written permission from the author, except for the use of brief quotations in a book review.

Made in the USA
Columbia, SC
05 April 2022